FUN WITH FESTIVALS

NOTES ON THE CONTRIBUTORS

Subhamoy Das is a journalist turned marketing and communication professional based in Delhi NCR. He is arguably one of India's first professional bloggers, having started blogging for About.com in 1999. As a columnist and author, he has worked with the New York Times Company, *Hindustan Times* and the India Today Group, has co-authored a bestselling book on Hinduism, and contributed to several books published by Hachette India.

Sulaiman Ahmad retired as a senior banking executive after working for four decades. He began his career as a university lecturer, moved to banking, travelled to more than thirty countries and finally returned to a writer's life. A degree in English literature and a classical education in Urdu-Persian have given him an acute understanding of both literary traditions. He took a three-year assignment as a visiting professor at Jamia Millia in their academy of international affairs. He has also authored three books – two in English and one an anthology of Urdu ghazals.

FUN WITH FESTIVALS

Stories by
SUBHAMOY DAS
and SULAIMAN AHMAD

Illustrated by
Shamika Chaves

hachette INDIA

First published in 2024 by Hachette India
(Registered name: Hachette Book Publishing India Pvt. Ltd)
An Hachette UK company
www.hachetteindia.com

1

ISBN 978-93-5731-781-8

Hachette Book Publishing India Pvt. Ltd
4th & 5th Floors, Corporate Centre
Plot No. 94, Sector 44, Gurugram – 122003, India

Typeset by Manmohan Kumar, Delhi

MIX
Paper | Supporting responsible forestry
FSC® C010615
FSC www.fsc.org

Printed and bound in India
by Thomson Press India Ltd.

CONTENTS

LOHRI

Come January and people in the northern Indian states of Punjab, Haryana and parts of Himachal Pradesh are busy preparing for Lohri – the long-awaited bonfire festival. It falls on the day before the festival of Makar Sankranti is celebrated in the rest of India.

Significance of This Harvest Festival

In Punjab, the breadbasket of India, wheat is the main winter crop. It is sown in October and harvested in March or April. In January, the fields come up with the promise of a golden harvest, and farmers celebrate Lohri during this rest period before the cutting and gathering of crop.

According to the Hindu calendar, Lohri falls in mid-January. This time ends the coldest month of the year, Paush, and the month of Magh starts. This is the auspicious period of Uttarayan. According to the Bhagavad Gita, Lord Krishna manifests himself in his full magnificence during this time.

On the morning of Lohri day, children go from door to door singing and demanding the Lohri 'loot' in the form of money and edibles such as *til* (sesame) seeds, peanuts, jaggery, or sweets such as *gajak, rewri*, etc. They sing in praise of Dulla Bhatti, the Punjabi avatar of Robin Hood, who robbed the rich to help the poor.

The Bonfire Ritual

With the setting of the sun in the evening, huge bonfires are lit in the harvested fields and in the front yards of houses. People gather around the rising flames, circle around the bonfire and throw puffed rice, popcorn and other munchies into the fire. While doing so, they shout *Aadar aye dilather jaye!* (May honor come and poverty vanish!), and sing popular folk songs. This is a sort of prayer to the fire god, to bless the land with abundance and prosperity.

After the *parikrama*, people meet friends and relatives, exchange greetings and gifts and distribute *prasad.* (offerings made to God). The *prasad* comprises five main items: *til, gajak,* jaggery, peanuts and popcorn. Winter savories are served around the bonfire with the traditional dinner of *makki-di-roti* (multi-millet hand-rolled bread) and *sarson-da-saag* (mustard greens).

Bhangra by men begins after the offering to the bonfire. Dancing continues until late night. Traditionally, women do not join the dance. Instead, they hold a separate bonfire in their courtyard and perform the *gidda* dance.

The day following Lohri is called Maghi. It signifies the beginning of the month of Magh. According to Hindu beliefs, this is an auspicious day to take a holy dip in the river and give to charity. Sweet dishes (usually *kheer*) are prepared with sugar cane juice to mark the day.

An Exhibition of Exuberance

Lohri is more than just a festival, especially for the people of Punjab. It offers an opportunity for people in the community to take a break from their busy schedule and get together to share each other's company. In other parts of India, Lohri almost coincides with the festivals of Pongal, Makar Sankranti and Uttarayan. All these festivals communicate the same message of oneness and celebrate the spirit of brotherhood.

ACTIVITIES

1 NO TRICK, ONLY TREAT

Trick or Treat with Punjabi clothes and sweets.

You Need:

- Traditional clothing (Pathani kurta, Patiala salwar suit, etc.)
- Gift bags • Lohri sweets

Celebrate It!

1) Plan the event with your neighbours and friends.
2) Kids should dress up in traditional Punjabi attire.
3) All families should keep sweets such as *gajak*, *rewri*, gur and even small packets of *gajar ka halwa* ready.
4) When the kids go knocking on different doors, each one of them must receive a token of festive sweetness.

2 FUN WITH POPCORN

Popcorn is a beloved snack during Lohri. Before you munch on them, you can always include them in a fun game.

You Need:

• Unpopped popcorn (popcorn kernel) • Small straws • Cousins or friends • Two bowls

Play It!

1) Keep the unpopped popcorn in one bowl and leave the other bowl empty.
2) Touch one popcorn kernel with one end of the straw. Place the other end in your mouth.
3) Suck the air in and pick the kernel up using only the straw. Do not touch the kernels with your hands.
4) One by one, move the kernels to the empty bowl.
5) See which one of your cousins or friends can move the highest number of kernels.

3 GROUNDNUTS FOR THE WIN

Collect all members of your family for a fun game with groundnuts.

You Need:

• Groundnuts or Peanuts (with their shells on) • Bowls

Play It!

1) Give one bowl to each participant.

2) Keep all the groundnuts in the centre so everyone can reach them.
3) The participants have to break the shells with one hand and keep the peanuts in their bowls.
4) The person who can extract the highest number of peanuts wins.
5) You can also change the rules and replace groundnut shells with simple peanut peels. Anyone who can peel off the most peanuts with one hand will win.

4 LOHRI QUIZ

Test your knowledge of the festival with some multiple-choice questions. Tick the correct answer.

1) Which traditional dance form is associated with Lohri?
   a) Garba
   b) Bharatanatyam
   c) Bhangra
   d) Kuchipudi
2) Pick a popular main course dish likely to be served at a Lohri dinner.
   a) Sambhar vada
   b) Sarson-da-saag
   c) Biryani
   d) Puran poli
3) A lot of Lohri songs commemorate which of the following figures?
   a) Dulla Bhatti
   b) Gugga Pir

c) Khetarpal
d) Guru Nanak Dev

4) Find the odd one out with respect to Lohri's *prasad.*
   a) Gur
   b) Peanuts
   c) Bananas
   d) Gajak

5 CLASSROOM DÉCOR

If your teacher agrees to it, band up with your classmates to decorate your class noticeboard the Lohri way.

You Need:

• Punch papers • Yellow, orange and brown paint • Paintbrush • A pair of scissors

Make It!

1) Each child gets one punch paper for the activity.
2) Dip either one of your palms in yellow or orange paint.
3) Place your palms on the punch paper.
4) Paint brown wood logs under this imprint.
5) Cut the shape of the bonfire out.
6) Pin or staple all the bonfire shapes on the noticeboard as a kind of background decoration.

Answers:
1) c, 2) b, 3) a, 4) c

PONGAL

Pongal is a festival that is celebrated every year in mid-January – mostly in the south of India and especially in Tamil Nadu. It marks the harvest of crops and offers a special thanksgiving to God, the sun, the Earth, and the cattle.

Pongal comes from the word 'ponga,' which literally means 'boil'. So, the word 'pongal' connotes that which is 'overflowing'. It's also the name of the special sweet dish cooked on Pongal day. Pongal continues through the first four days of the Thai month (tenth month as per the traditional Tamil year) that starts on 14 January every year.

Seasonal Harvest Festivity

Pongal is directly associated with the annual cycle of seasons. It not only marks the reaping of the harvest but also the withdrawal of the southeast monsoons in southern India.

Each day of the four-day festival has its own name and distinct fashion of celebration.

Day 1: Bhogi Pongal

Bhogi Pongal is a day for the family, for domestic activities. This day is celebrated in honour of Lord Indra, 'the ruler of clouds and the giver of rains'.

On the first day of Pongal, a huge bonfire is lit at dawn in front of the house, and all old and useless items are set ablaze. It symbolises the beginning of a fresh new year. The bonfire burns through the night as people beat drums and dance around it. Homes are cleaned and decorated with *kolam* – floor designs drawn with rice paste. Often, pumpkin flowers are set into cow-dung balls and placed among the patterns.

Day 2: Surya Pongal

The second day is dedicated to Lord Surya, the Sun God, who is offered boiled milk and jaggery. A plank is placed on the ground. A large image of the Sun God is sketched on it, and *kolam* designs are drawn around it.

Day 3: Mattu Pongal

This third day is meant for the *mattu* (cattle). They are given a good bath, their horns are polished, painted and covered with metal caps, and garlands are put around their necks. The pongal that has been offered to the gods is then given to the cattle to eat. They are then taken out to the racing tracks for cattle race and bullfight – Jallikattu – an event full of festivity and fun.

Day 4: Kanya Pongal

The fourth and final day marks the Kanya Pongal when birds are worshipped. Coloured balls of cooked rice are kept in the open for birds and fowls to eat. On this day sisters also pray for their brothers' happiness.

Like all festivals, Pongal also has some interesting legends attached to it.

The Mount Govardhan Tale

The most popular Pongal legend is the one associated with the first day of the celebrations when Lord Indra is worshipped. On this day, Indra became proud and arrogant. To teach him a lesson, Lord Krishna asked his cowherd friends to worship Mount Govardhan instead of Indra on the Bhogi Pongal day. An angry Indra sent forth the clouds to generate thunder, lightning and heavy rains. But Lord Krishna lifted up the Govardhan Mountain on his little finger and sheltered the farmers, cowherd and their cattle. Indra then begged for Krishna's forgiveness and the latter re-permitted Bhogi Pongal celebrations in honour of Indra.

The Nandi Bull Story

According to another legend, on the third day of celebrations, Lord Shiva once asked his bull, Nandi, to go to Earth and deliver a special message to his disciples: 'Have an oil bath every day and food once a month.'

But the baffled bull failed to deliver the correct message. Instead, he told the people that Shiva asked them to 'have an oil bath once a month and food every day'. The enraged Shiva then ordered Nandi to stay back on Earth and help the people plow the fields since they would now need to grow more grains, due to his mistake.

ACTIVITIES

1 PONGAL POT DÉCOR

Use your artistry to cultivate a colourful Pongal.

You Need:

• An earthen or brass pot • Acrylic paints
• Paint brushes • A bowl of water • One or two turmeric shoot/s

Make It!

1) Coat your pot with a layer of white paint. It will serve as a base for your creativity.
2) You may use red paint to colour the pot's mouth and yellow to draw horizontal lines around its body, or vice versa.
3) Use green to draw leaves emerging from the yellow/red lines.
4) You are free to choose the pattern of the leaves.
5) Use a bright colour like pink or orange to paint small flowers between or on the edges of the leaves.

6) Tie and knot the turmeric shoot/s around the neck of your Pongal Pot. It is now ready to carry your Pongal dish!

2 PAINT THE FLOORS WHITE

Learn how to make easy *kolam* patterns with a basic knowledge of geometry.

You Need:

- Rice flour

Make It!

1) The most beginner-friendly way to design a *kolam* is to use geometrical shapes.
2) Use your index finger and thumb to draw a simple square or diamond on the floor.

3) Make a small circle at the centre of your shape.
4) Fill the circle with smaller concentric circles or a circular spiral.
5) See what other shapes you can use to decorate the boundary of your square/diamond.
6) You may use triangles, semi-circles, dots, straight lines or free-hand patterns like flower petals and leaves.
7) Once you are done, show your *kolam* to an adult and ask them about its importance in Pongal festivities.

3 VEN PONGAL

Like any other festival, Pongal is incomplete without its savoury festivities.

You Need:

• ¼ cup roasted moong lentils • ½ cup rice
• Cumin seeds • Chopped ginger • Salt
• Cashews • Black pepper • Curry leaves
• Pressure cooker • Bowls

Make It!

1) Ask an adult to roast moong lentils beforehand.
2) Add rice to the bowl of roasted moong lentils and rinse the mixture with warm water.
3) Make sure you drain the water properly.
4) Put the mixture in a pressure cooker.
5) Add cumin seeds, chopped ginger, salt and other spices. Let an adult oversee the quantity of the spices.

6) Pour two to three cups of water and pressure cook on medium heat. Let an adult manage the cooking.
7) For a flavourful dressing, you can help fry some cashews with black pepper and curry leaves and pour it on top of the Ven Pongal.
8) Serve the Ven Pongal hot and delicious!

4 DIY NEWSPAPER SUGARCANE

There is always time for some festival crafts!

You Need:

• Old newspapers • Paintbrush
• Dark and light green paint • A pair of scissors • Glue

Make It!

1) Take one half of a single newspaper sheet and fold it further in half.
2) Fold about three inches in from one side and then open it. Let there be a visible line where you have folded the page.
3) Paint this three-inch strip dark green on both sides.
4) Use light green paint to highlight the visible line. This will form the lower part of your sugarcane leaves.
5) Cut long leaves out of the green strip but do not remove it from the rest of the newspaper sheet.
6) Let it dry!
7) After a few minutes, start rolling the newspaper sheet diagonally from one unpainted corner.

8) Use glue to stick the free end onto the 'stem'.
9) Colour the remaining parts of your handmade sugarcane with light green paint.

5 TWIST URI ADITHAL

While the traditional game of Pongal is played outdoors and is mostly for adults, you can always make your own set of rules and play it indoors.

You Need:

- A group of six to seven kids
- Three earthen pots
- A safe indoor space
- Blindfolds

Play It!

1) Make three (or more) pairs from the given group of kids, including yourself.
2) One person in each pair has to be blindfolded.
3) Arrange earthen pots on a table or similar surface, one pot for each pair.
4) Decide on another empty table or surface which will serve as a victory point.
5) The objective of every pair is to transfer their earthen pot from the first table to the victory point. The blindfolded person will do this while their partner guides them across the room.
6) Be safe and have fun!

VASANT PANCHAMI

As Diwali is to Lakshmi, goddess of wealth and prosperity, and Navaratri is to Durga, goddess of power and valour, the day of Vasant Panchami is an ode to Saraswati, the goddess of knowledge and arts. This festival is celebrated every year on the fifth day or Panchami of the bright fortnight of the lunar month of Magh, which falls during January–February. 'Vasant' comes from the word 'spring' as this festival heralds the beginning of the spring season.

Birthday of Goddess Saraswati

It is believed that on this day, Goddess Saraswati was born. Statues of the goddess are ritually worshipped and offered sweets which are given away as prasad to the devotees. There is also a custom of ancestor worship, known as Pitri-Tarpan in many parts of India during Vasant Panchami.

Saraswati's favourite colour, yellow, assumes special significance on this day. It symbolizes both the goddess' wisdom and the vibrancy of spring. Devotees adorn themselves and their homes in yellow, offering yellow flowers and sweets as symbols of knowledge and the rising sun.

The Symbolism of Saraswati

Saraswati, the goddess of knowledge, music, art, wisdom, and nature, represents the free flow of wisdom and consciousness. She is the mother of the Vedas. The chants directed to her, called the Saraswati Vandana, often begin and end Vedic lessons.

It is believed that goddess Saraswati endows human beings with the powers of speech, wisdom and learning. She has four hands representing four aspects of human personality in learning: mind, intellect, alertness and ego. In visual representations, she has sacred scriptures in one hand and a lotus, the symbol of true knowledge, in the opposite hand. With her other two hands, Saraswati plays the music of love and life on a string instrument called the veena. She is dressed in white – the symbol of purity – and rides on a white swan, symbolizing Sattva Guna (purity and discrimination).

The Foundation of Education

The most significant aspect of Vasant Panchami is that it is also the most auspicious day to begin laying one's foundations of education – of how to read and write. Pre-school children are given their first lesson in reading and writing on this day. It is also a great day to inaugurate training institutes and new schools – a trend made famous by the renowned Indian educationist Pandit Madan Mohan Malaviya (1861–1946), who founded the Banaras Hindu University on Vasant Panchami day in 1916.

Vasant Panchami also announces the arrival of another significant springtime event in the Hindu calendar – Holi.

Saraswati Vandana – Sanskrit Hymn for Vasant Panchami

The following hymn is also recited on Vasant Panchami:

Yaa Kundendu tushaara haaradhavalaa, Yaa shubhravastraavritha|

Yaa veenavara dandamanditakara, Yaa shwetha padmaasana||

Yaa brahmaachyutha shankara prabhritibhir Devaisadaa Venditha|

Saa Maam Paatu Saraswatee Bhagavatee Nihshesha jaadyaapahaa||

May Goddess Saraswati,
who is fair like the jasmine-coloured moon,
and whose pure white garland is like frosty dew drops;
who is adorned in radiant white attire,
on whose beautiful arm rests the veena,
and whose throne is a white lotus;
who is surrounded and respected by the Gods, protect me.
May you fully remove my lethargy, sluggishness, and ignorance.

ACTIVITIES

1 DONATION DRIVE

To commemorate the goddess of knowledge, plan a drive to donate educational material to people in need.

You Need:

- Books you don't use anymore
- Notebooks • Pencils and pens • Other stationery

Use the web to get information about orphanages and NGOs near you. You can also ask your family, neighbours and schoolteachers for recommendations.

Convince some of your friends or classmates to join you in the activity. Contact the orphanage or NGO to share your objective with them before you visit.

2 SWEET RICE

Help prepare a saffron-infused sweet rice meal to celebrate spring's arrival. The ingredients below are enough for one person.

You Need:

• 1 cup basmati rice • Ghee • Milk
• 1 piece of cinnamon stick • Sugar
• Cardamom (whole or crushed) • Salt
• Almonds (crushed) • Raisins
• Cloves • Saffron

Make It!

1) Ask an adult to roast the almonds and raisins beforehand.
2) Cook the rice with salt and cinnamon stick.
3) Mix sugar, ghee, milk, saffron, cloves and cardamom in a separate cooking utensil. Let an adult help you with the measurements.
4) Boil until the sugar dissolves. This is your sugar syrup.
5) Add the roasted nuts and syrup to the rice.
6) Let it cook for a few minutes on low heat and serve hot.

3 BALLET OF SWANS

Learn about goddess Saraswati with nothing but your pencils and crayons.

You Need:

• A drawing notebook or sketchbook
• Pencils and colours

Make It!

1) To sketch a simple swan, draw the digit '2' with its horizontal line curved slightly to resemble a wave.

2) Draw a rounded mouth, a long neck and a body.
3) Draw a few slanted strokes towards the swan's tail to resemble wings.
4) Add a beak and an eye.
5) You can colour the background to make your swan stand out.
6) Draw multiple swans and work with your own creativity to make each one look unique.

4 PAINT IT YELLOW!

Bask in the glow of your handmade sunflowers.

You Need:

• Yellow tissue paper • Stapler
• Cotton balls • Brown paint • Glue

Make It!

1) Stack two tissue paper squares.
2) Fold them in half four times.

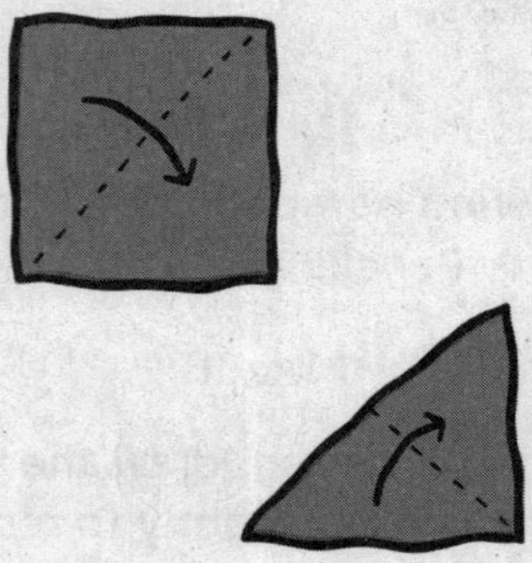

3) Cut the wider part of the folded paper into the shape of a petal. The petal's head should be semi-circular.
4) Open it up and repeat with the other pair of tissue squares.
5) Stick all the tissue flowers together from their centres. Make sure you can see the petals of one flower from the gaps of another.
6) Tear out a small cotton ball and dip it in brown paint.
7) Stick it onto your sunflower's centre.
8) Make as many sunflowers as you want and use them to decorate your room.

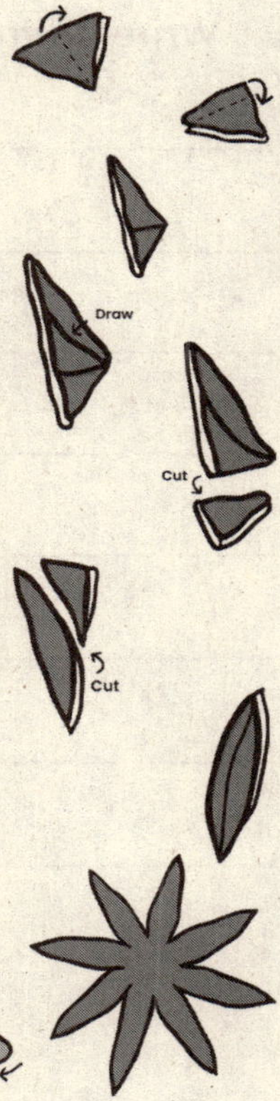

5 CREATOR OF WORDS

Gather your friends and grab a few pens. See who can create the maximum number of words from the letters in VASANT PANCHAMI.

Write down the words you come up with below:

MAHA SHIVRATRI

Maha Shivratri, the night of the worship of Lord Shiva, occurs on the fourteenth night of the new moon during the dark half of the month of Phalguna. It falls on a moonless February night, when devotees offer special prayer to the lord of destruction. Shivratri (in Sanskrit, 'ratri' means night) is the night when Lord Shiva is said to have performed the *Tandava Nritya* – the dance of creation, preservation and destruction. The festival is observed for one day and one night only.

When Shiva Saved the World

Maha Shivratri commemorates the wedding of Shiva and Parvati. Legends have it that Lord Shiva tied the nuptial knot with Parvati on this day.

According to ancient Indian scriptures called the Puranas, during the great mythical churning of the ocean called *Samudra Manthan*, a pot of poison emerged from the ocean. The gods and the demons were terrified, as it could destroy the entire world. When they ran to Shiva for help, he drank the deadly poison to protect the world.

But he held it in his throat instead of swallowing it. This turned his throat blue, and because of this he came to be known as Nilkantha, the blue-throated one. According to this mythical tale, Shivratri is celebrated to mark the day when Shiva saved the world.

Shiva and the Origin of the Ganga

A legend from the Ramayana speaks of King Bhagirath, who once meditated before Lord Brahma for a thousand years for the salvation of the souls of his ancestors. Pleased with his devotion, Brahma granted him a wish. The king then requested that the Lord send the river goddess Ganga down to Earth from heaven so that she could flow over his ancestors' ashes and wash their curse away.

Brahma granted his wish but requested that the king first pray to Shiva, for Shiva alone could support the weight of Ganga's descent. Accordingly, King Bhagirath prayed to Shiva, who agreed. After travelling down through Shiva's thick matted locks, the river Ganga appeared on Earth. Today, this legend is re-enacted by a ceremonial ritual known as bathing the Shiva Lingam.

Shivratri Rituals

On the day of Shivratri, a three-tiered platform is built around a fire. The topmost plank represents heaven, the middle one space and the bottom one Earth. Eleven *kalash*, or urns, are kept on the plank, symbolizing the eleven manifestations of the 'Rudra' or destructive Shiva. These are decorated with the leaves of *bilva* or *bael* and mango atop a coconut representing the head of Shiva. The uncut shank of the coconut symbolizes his tangled hair and the three spots on the fruit, Shiva's three eyes.

The symbol representing Shiva is called the *lingam,* which is usually made of granite, soapstone, quartz, marble or metal. It is bathed every three hours with the five sacred offerings of a cow, called the *panchagavya* – milk, sour milk, urine, butter and dung.

All through the day, the devotees fast and chant 'Om Namah Shivaya' and make offerings of flowers and incense to Shiva. They maintain long vigils during the night and listen to stories, hymns and songs. The fast is broken only the next morning.

ACTIVITIES

1 SHIVA'S DAMARU

Craft a mini *damaru* before the festivities begin!

You Need:

• 2 plastic bottles • Beading thread
• 2 small beads • Paper cutter • A pair of scissors
• Transparent or white tape • Glue
• Sheets of white and black paper • Brown paint
• Paintbrush

Make It!

1) Place the bottles vertically on a flat surface. You have to work with the top portions of the bottles from where they begin to taper towards the cap.
2) With the help of an adult, cut these top portions out.
3) Loosen the caps and tape together the mouths of the two plastic pieces.
4) This is the body of your *damaru*. Use brown paint to colour the outside of it.

5) Cut out two big white circles to make the two heads of the *damaru.*
6) Once the glue is dry, remove the excess bit of paper.
7) Cut two smaller black circles and attach them to the centres of the white circles.
8) Take 15 inches of a beading thread and attach two small beads on both ends of it. Secure the beads with knots.
9) Tie this thread around the middle part of the *damaru*, making multiple rounds. Keep a few centimetres on both ends free.
10) You can now shake the Damaru and see the beads dance around!

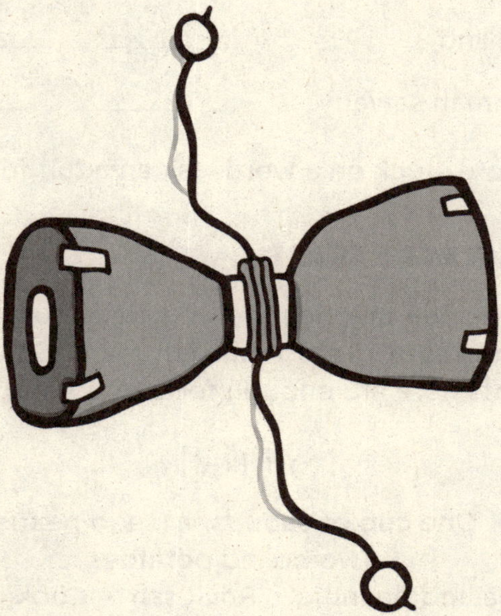

2 SHIVRATRI WORD SCRAMBLE

Keeping in mind all that you have learnt about the festival and other things you may know, try to unscramble these words:

1) vnatada ______________________
2) muotn haikalsa ______________________
3) amadaehv ______________________
4) vpairat ______________________
5) slhvgini ______________________
6) tadihan ______________________
7) otlebhanh ______________________
8) mo ahman saivahy ______________________

If you are stuck on a word, ask an adult for help.

3 SHIVRATRI FEAST

Fasting recipes are healthy and delicious. *Sabudana khichdi* makes a great meal for Maha Shivratri. The ingredients here are enough for one person.

You Need:

- One cup of *sabudana* (sago pearls)
- Two boiled potatoes
- Roasted peanuts • Rock salt • Cooking oil

Make It!

1) Ask an adult to boil/roast the ingredients as mentioned beforehand.
2) Rinse and soak *sabudana* overnight. Drain it well.
3) Peel and chop the potatoes.
4) Using a blender, grind the peanuts till they are almost powdery.
5) Add them to the *sabudana*. Sprinkle in some rock salt.
6) Mix the ingredients.
7) Here, let an adult cook the potatoes in some oil. Add spices as per your liking.
8) Add in the *sabudana*-peanut mixture and cook it for about five minutes on low heat. Stir at regular intervals.
9) Garnish and serve it hot.

4 HEALTH-CONSCIOUS SHIVRATRI

Get together with your loved ones and participate in this meditative tradition.

You Need:

- Yoga mats

Celebrate It!

1) Stand upright with your feet close together but not touching.
2) Extend your arms towards the front and interlock your fingers. Your palms should be facing away from your body.

3) Inhale and lift your arms above your head.
4) At the same time, raise your heels.
5) This is called Tadasana. Relax and then repeat it as many times as you want.
6) After that, try standing on one leg.
7) Bend the knee of your other leg. Let the sole of your foot rest against the standing leg.
8) Join your palms above your head in a prayer-like position. This is called Vrikshasana.
9) Practice and include other such poses for a calming and mindful session.

5 FIND THE IMPOSTERS

The following sets contain some names of Lord Shiva. However, some of these names do not belong here. See if you can figure them out.

1) Mahesha, Meghavahana, Rudra, Neelakanta, Vinata
2) Daksha, Mahadeva, Shambhu, Narada, Shankara

Answers:
1) Tandava, 2) Mount Kailasha, 3) Mahadeva, 4) Parvati, 5) Shivling, 6) Thandai, 7) Bholenath, 8) Om Namah Shivaya

Answers:
1) Meghavahana, Vinata
2) Daksha, Narada

HOLI

Holi, the festival of colours, is undoubtedly the most fun-filled of Indian festivals. It is an occasion that brings in pure joy and cheer, fun and play, music and dance, and, of course, lots and lots of bright colours!

With winter neatly tucked away in the attic, it is time to come out of our cocoons and enjoy this spring festival. Every year, Holi is celebrated on the day after the full moon in early March and glorifies a good harvest and the fertility of the land. New crops are reaped and granaries are reloaded across shops and households. It is perhaps such abundance that accounts for the merriment during Holi.

THE MYTHS OF HOLI

Like most Indian festivals, Holi is linked to mythical tales featuring warriors, gods, demonesses and *asura*s. There are at least four legends that are directly associated with the festival of colours: the Holika-Hiranyakashipu-Prahlada episode, Lord Shiva's killing of Kamadeva, the story of the ogress Dhundhi, and the Lord Krishna legend. In most of these stories, good defeats evil forces and Holi is a part of the resulting celebration that follows.

A Wicked Demoness is Burnt Alive

The evolution of the term Holi makes for an interesting study in itself. Legend has it that Holi derives its name from Holika, the sister of the mythical king Hiranyakashipu who commanded everyone to worship him.. But his young son, Prahlada, refused to do so as he was a devout follower of Vishnu, the preserver of the universe.

Hiranyakashipu, angered by his son's disobedience, ordered his sister Holika to kill Prahlada. She possessed the power to walk through fire unharmed. So she picked up Prahlada and walked into a fire with him. Prahlada, however, chanted the many names of Lord Vishnu and was saved from the fire. Holika perished because she did not know that her powers were only effective if she entered the fire alone.

Today, people follow the practice of creating a pyre the night before Holi. They set fire to it as a symbol of the burning of Holika. This is known as Holika Dahan.

The God of Love is Worshipped

It is often believed that it was on Holi that Lord Shiva opened his third eye and burned Kamadeva, the god of love, to ashes. This happened when Shiva was disturbed during his meditation. It is one of the reasons why many people worship Kamadeva on Holi, with a simple offering of a mixture of mango blossoms and sandalwood paste.

An Ogress is Defeated by Children

It was also on this day that an ogress called Dhundhi, who was troubling children in the kingdom of Prithu, was chased away by the shouts and pranks of village youngsters. Although this female monster had secured several boons that made her almost unbeatable, the shouts, abuses and pranks of the boys defeated her. This was a weakness for Dhundhi, because of a curse from Lord Shiva. The little boys took advantage of her weakness and drove her out of their land.

Krishna Plays Holi with the Gopis

In the legends of Krishna as a youth, he is seen as playing all sorts of pranks with the *gopis*, or female cowherds. One prank was to throw coloured powder all over them. So, on Holi, images of Krishna are often carried through the streets. Holi is celebrated with great vigour in the villages around Mathura, the birthplace of Krishna. Holi is also associated with the divine dance known as Raaslila staged by Lord Krishna for the benefit of his devout *gopis*.

HOLI DOWN THE AGES

Holi as a festival seems to have started several centuries back. It has been mentioned in the religious works of Jaimini's *Purvamimasa-Sutras* and *Kathaka-Grhya-Sutra*.

Holi in Temple Sculptures

Holi is one of the oldest among Hindu festivals. Various references are found in the sculptures on walls of old temples, such as the sixteenth-century panel sculpted in a temple in Hampi, Karnataka. It shows a prince and his princess standing among maids, waiting to soak the royal couple in coloured water.

Birthday of Shri Chaitanya Mahaprabhu

Holi Purnima is also celebrated as the birthday of Shri Chaitanya Mahaprabhu (a sixteenth-century Vaishnava saint and social reformer), mostly in Bengal, Orissa and the holy cities of Mathura and Vrindavan in the state of Uttar Pradesh.

The Ancient Colours of Holi

The colours of Holi, called *gulal*, were made at home in the medieval times from flowers of the Tesu or Palash tree, also called 'the flame of the forest'. These flowers, bright-red or deep-orange in colour, were collected from the forest and spread out on mats to dry in the sun, and then ground to fine dust. The powder, when mixed with water, made a beautiful saffron-red dye. This colour and also *abeer*, made from natural coloured talc, which were extensively used as Holi colours earlier. They were good for the skin, unlike modern chemical colours.

CELEBRATING HOLI

Colourful days, serious rituals, joyous celebrations – Holi is a lively occasion! Aside from the colour revelry, there is an exchange of greetings, the elders distribute sweets and money, and all join in an enthusiastic dance to the rhythm of the drums.

Holi: Day 1

The day of the full moon (Holi Purnima) is the first day of Holi. A platter (thali) is arranged with coloured powders (*gulal*), and coloured water is placed in a small brass pot (*lota*). The eldest male member of the family begins the festivities by sprinkling colours on each member of the family and the youngsters follow.

Holi: Day 2

On the second day of the festival called 'Puno', images of Holika are burnt in keeping with the legend of Prahlada and his devotion to Lord Vishnu. In rural India, the evening is celebrated by lighting huge bonfires as part of a community event. People gather near the fire and celebrate Holika Dahan with folk songs and dances.

Holi: Day 3

The most boisterous day is the final one of the festival called 'Parva', when children, youth, men and women visit each other's homes and coloured powders called *abeer* and *gulal* are thrown in the air and smeared on each other's faces and bodies. *Pichkari*s and water balloons are filled with colours and squirted onto people.

A NATURAL HOLI

Have you ever wondered how to make the festival of colours natural and healthy for our environment and ourselves? Did you know that Holi can be fun and harmless if you play with environment-friendly natural colours? These are not only inexpensive but can also be made easily at home.

Explore the fascinating world of natural colours. Experiment with different flowers, fruits and vegetables (like black grapes and dried fruits such as *amla*/gooseberry), leaves (eucalyptus) and plants (*arandi*/castor). Encourage the use of eco-friendly natural colours and motivate your friends to do so as well.

Save Your Skin from Chemical Colours

Most Holi colours sold in the market are oxidized metals or industrial dyes mixed with engine oil. Green comes from copper sulphate, purple is chromium iodide, silver is aluminium bromide, black is lead oxide and shiny colours are a result of powdered glass being added to the colours. All these are toxic and can result in skin allergies, eye irritation, blindness and much more.

When washed, they enter the rivers and the soil and increase pollution.

Play Holi the Vedic Way

By using safe and natural colours, we not only save our skins but also help save our environment and conserve our biodiversity. When these natural colours drain through into the soil and water, they do not poison our blue planet. They also do not harm the various life forms that live in the soil and water. Thereby, we also preserve the diverse plants and trees that give us these colours and live life the Vedic way, which is a simple, natural and spiritual way of existence.

ACTIVITIES

1 BALLOON PEOPLE

Bring your balloons to life by creating your own colourful balloon people!

You Need:

- Balloons • Coloured paper • Pencil • A pair of scissors
- Decorative items (glitter, coloured pens, googly eyes)

Make It!

1) Blow up a balloon and tie it up.
2) On a piece of coloured paper, draw the outline of the shoes/skirt/etc., which your balloon person will wear, in pencil.
3) Cut out the item and poke a hole in the centre for the tied end of the balloon to fit through.
4) Decorate the balloon (draw on a face, stick on eyes and ears).
5) Pull the tied end of the balloon through the hole that you made earlier.

6) Add final touches of decoration.
7) Your balloon person is ready for display.

2 MAKE YOUR OWN HOLIKA

Create your own Holika that can melt in a fire!

You Need:

• 1¼ cups salt • 1¼ cups flour • ¾ cup water
• Paints • Mixing bowl

Make It!

1) Mix the salt and flour together in a large bowl.
2) Create a well in the middle of the mix.
3) Gradually add water. If the dough becomes too sticky, add more flour. If it is too crumbly, add more water.
4) Form the dough into a ball and knead it until it is smooth enough to use.
5) Now you are ready to create your Holika. Mould the dough with your hands into the form you want.
6) Decorate it using paints and powders. Now toss it into a bonfire and watch it melt away.

3 SPECIAL HOLI KULFI

No festival is complete without a sweet ending. Make this special kulfi with the help of an adult and watch your Holi celebrations get sweeter.

You Need:

• 500 ml full cream milk • ¼ cup milk powder
• ½ cup sweetened condensed milk • ¼ cup sugar
• 4 green cardamom seeds (finely powdered)
• Food colour (red, green, yellow)

Make It!

1) Boil the milk, milk powder, condensed milk and sugar together.
2) Once it has boiled, add the powdered cardamom.
3) Let it cook for 10 minutes on medium heat. Make sure you have an adult to help you.
4) Turn off the gas and let it cool completely.
5) Divide into three separate bowls and mix in a few drops of different food colours in each.
6) Pour your coloured mixture into moulds (you can use kulfi moulds, glasses, trays, or anything you wish).
7) Freeze overnight till firm.
8) Before serving, allow the moulds to remain outside for five minutes and then take it out of the moulds.
9) Enjoy your brightly coloured special Holi kulfi.

4 HOLI DIP POOL

You Need:

• An inflatable kiddie pool • Water • Flowers
• Coloured powder • A long twig or wooden stick

Make It!

1) Fill up the kiddie pool with water.
2) Sprinkle flowers and a little bit of powder in it.
3) Give it a stir with the twig to mix the colours and flowers with the water.
4) Jump in!

5 CREATE YOUR OWN PICHKARI

You Need:

• Old spray bottles • Acrylic paints • Glitter • Water • Coloured powder

Make It!

1) Decorate your old spray bottles using your imagination. Go wild with the paints and glitter.
2) Fill it up with coloured water and spread the joy!

6 AN ECO-WARRIOR'S HOLI ARSENAL

Instead of buying synthetic colours which may have harmful chemicals, why not make your own eco-friendly colours at home and become a super eco-warrior? We have a few easy ideas to help you stock up your arsenal this Holi!

Ravishing Reds

You Need:

• Red Hibiscus flowers • Flour

Make It!

1) Dry the red Hibiscus flowers in the shade.
2) Crush it into a powder to make a lovely red colour.
3) To get more powder add some flour to it, but be careful not to add too much otherwise you will ruin the colour!

Garden Greens

You Need:

- Henna powder (not the variety that says it is mixed with amla) • Flour

Make It!

1) Mix the henna powder with an equal quantity of flour.
2) Go ahead and play with this without any fear as dry henna will not leave colour on your face.

7 TIE-DYE

What better Holi outfit than your very own handcrafted tie-and-dye t-shirt. You can use organic colours to create tie-and-dye patterns that fit perfectly with Holi's colourful theme.

You Need:

- Vegetables (tomatoes, carrots, beetroot or spinach)
- Fruits (strawberries, cherries, blueberries or *jamun*)

• Flowers (marigolds, blue hibiscus, Tesu flowers)
• Knife • Pot • Water • Strainer • Light-coloured cotton clothes • Vinegar • Rubber bands
• Wooden spoon • Rubber gloves

Make It!

Note: Ask an adult to help you with this.

Step 1: Making the Dye

1) Collect your plant material and chop it up, or peel the fruits. Take the skins/peel and recycle the rest (eat the fruits and vegetables, or ask an adult to cook up a yummy dish with them).
2) Place the skins in a pot of water. You should use two parts water for one part of peel.
3) Let it boil for one to four hours. The longer you simmer the plant/fruit and water, the deeper the shade will be.
4) Strain the water when cool and throw away the leftover peels. Store the dye in the refrigerator for up to seventy-two hours.

Step 2: Preparing the Fabric
1) Mix four parts cold water to one part vinegar in a pot.

2) Add your clothes to the pot. Remember, you don't just want the clothes to soak up all of the liquid – you want them swimming.

3) Leave the pot on the stove for one hour.
4) Rinse them in cold water, squeezing out excess moisture. Lay them out until slightly damp.

5) Tie the fabric in select areas with rubber bands to create the tie-dye effect.

Step 3: Dying the T-Shirt

1) Pour the dye in a pot. Add your t-shirt. Put it on the stove, stirring occasionally. Let it sit for at least one hour.

2) Remove the pot from the heat. Leave the fabric in the dye for another hour or two – or overnight. (Remember that the shade will be much lighter after rinsing than it looks in the dye pot).

3) Put on rubber gloves. Rinse out the fabric in the sink until the water runs clear.

4) Rinse the t-shirt in warm water and lay it out to dry in the air.
5) When it is still slightly damp, ask an adult to iron it to help set the colour.
6) Wash it in hot water before wearing it.

GOOD FRIDAY AND EASTER

On a weekend bathed in spring's gentle sunlight, Christian communities across the globe celebrate a festival steeped in sombre reflection, joyful celebration, and the unshakeable conviction in the promise of redemption and new beginnings. This is the festival of Good Friday and Easter that reflects the human heart's deepest yearnings for forgiveness, hope and transformation.

The Story of Jesus' Crucifixion and Good Friday

Two thousand years ago in Jerusalem, a young man named Jesus walked and taught people about the power of love. His followers loved his message of compassion and equality. But people who clung to power and tradition disliked Jesus. They accused Jesus of blasphemy – insulting religion – and sentenced him to death by crucifixion.

Good Friday falls on the Friday after the first full moon following the spring equinox – typically between 22 March and 25 April each year. It marks the end of Lent, a forty-day period of reflection, fasting, and preparation for the joyous celebration of Easter. Churches around the world play hymns and prayers, remembering the suffering of Jesus. In some traditions, processions carry crosses through the streets to mark the path Jesus walked on that fateful day.

The Resurrection and Promise of New Beginnings

Easter is celebrated on the Sunday following Good Friday. The Bible says that on the third day after Jesus' crucifixion, his tomb lay empty. The man who was killed had risen, alive and whole. This wasn't just a miracle but a victory over death itself.

Easter Eggs and Bunnies

The playful traditions of Easter eggs and bunnies hold deeper symbolic meanings. Eggs, representing new life, are often decorated and hidden. This symbolizes the joy of discovery and the hidden promise of Easter. Bunnies, known for their abundance, are associated with new beginnings. These playful symbols add an extra layer of joy and wonder to the celebration.

How Easter Is Celebrated Around the World

Easter is celebrated across the country. The St. Thomas Christians of Kerala take part in processions accompanied by the beats of *chenda* drums. Tribal communities in the

Northeast decorate churches with indigenous motifs. In Goa, churches like the Basilica of Bom Jesus host grand processions and light up displays.

Across the globe, Easter celebrations take on distinct forms. In Jerusalem, thousands of people participate in the Via Dolorosa pilgrimage. It retraces Jesus' steps to Golgotha. St. Peter's Square in Rome transforms into a sea of white as the Pope delivers his *Urbi et Orbi* ('to the city and the world') blessing on Easter Sunday. In Russia, midnight church services are held to mark the end of Lent. And in parts of Eastern Europe, burning bonfires on Easter Saturday symbolize the end of winter and the arrival of spring.

The Vatican, the centre of the Catholic Church, hosts a week of elaborate ceremonies culminating in Easter Sunday. On Good Friday, the Pope presides over the 'Way of the Cross' procession within the Colosseum. Easter Vigil on Saturday night features the lighting of the Easter candle, followed by a festive Mass on Easter Sunday, where the Pope delivers his message of hope and peace.

Easter's Message of Peace and Hope

Christians believe Easter, Good Friday and Easter Monday teach us to live out their message of love and compassion in our daily lives. The spirit of sacrifice reminds us of the power of giving and standing up for what is right. The joy of resurrection inspires us to embrace hope and overcome challenges. And the spirit of renewal calls us to shed the burdens of the past and embrace the potential for a new beginning.

ACTIVITIES

1 EASTER EGG WORD BUILDING

Gather your friends and organize an Easter Egg hunt that involves making words.

You Need:

- Plastic easter eggs • Punch papers
- Sketch pens • A pair of scissors

Play It!

1) Colour and cut out alphabet shapes off the punch sheets.
2) Keep these alphabets in separate easter eggs. If you have enough eggs, you can keep one alphabet in each. Otherwise, three to four in each egg will do.
3) Hide these eggs all over the place.
4) Set out for the hunt individually.
5) Try to find as many alphabets as you can and form words out of them.
6) The person who makes the most words wins.

2 FILL IN THE EGG

A fun activity that encourages you to be creative and artistic.

Draw an egg below and fill it up with patterns of your choice. Once you are satisfied with your design, colour it in. Show it to your family.

3 EASTER CANDY JAR

Prepare a handy container to store your favourite candy!

You Need:

• Mason jar (or a similar jar) • Coloured tissue paper
• Punch paper • Cotton • Glue
• A pair of scissors • Candy • Cello tape

Make It!

1) Draw bunny ears on a punch sheet and cut them out.
2) Glue bits of cotton on them to add a bunny texture.
3) Glue or tape them on the lid of the jar.
4) Fill the jar with candy.
5) Crumple up some tissue paper and line the jar's rim with it. Some part of the tissue should be outside and some inside the jar.
6) You don't need to stick the tissue with glue. Instead, simply put the lid back in place.
7) Keep the jar where everyone can see it.

4 EASTER FLOWER BASKET

Make a flower basket to gift to a loved one.

You Need:

• A coloured sheet of paper • Glue
• Flowers • Sketch pens

Make It!

1) Roll the coloured sheet of paper to make a large cone.
2) Glue the open flap in place.
3) Draw eyes and whiskers on one side of the conical basket.
4) You can also paste googly eyes if you have them.
5) Gently put some flowers in the basket and give it to someone you care about.

5 BUNNY UP!

Add a little Easter magic to your headband.

You Need:

- Punch paper • A pair of scissors • Glue
- Old fabric (preferably pink) • Cello tape
- Floral wire or coconut broom sticks
- A plastic headband

Make It!

1) Draw two bunny ears on a punch paper. Make sure their lower ends are narrow and long enough to wrap around the headband's width.
2) Cut out four ears of the same shape and size from a piece of coloured fabric.
3) If you have enough leftover fabric, you may even cover the headband with it to enhance the look of your bunny ears.

4) Glue two fabric ears onto the paper ears and let them dry.
5) Carefully attach the ears to the headband, with their lower strips glued around the plastic. Turn your headband over.
6) Use a piece of floral wire or broom stick to prepare a base so that your bunny ears don't droop.
7) Glue two wires or broom sticks vertically onto the headband on the paper-side of the ears.
8) Tape the sticks against the ears cleanly.
9) Cover it up with the two remaining fabric ears.
10) Let your headband dry before putting it on.

EID

RAMADAN AND EID: THE MEANING, THE DATE AND THE HISTORY

Ramadan: The Word and Its Meaning

Ramadan is the ninth month in the Islamic calendar. This month is considered holy by Muslims as they believe that their Holy Book, the Quran, was revealed by God to Prophet Mohammad during this month. It is the month of fasting, which represents complete devotion towards God and instils the qualities of patience and spirituality.

Ramadan is an Arabic word, which means scorching heat and dryness of the ground. In Urdu it is known as Ramzan. In Persian and Turkish it is called Ramazan. The month of fasting finally draws to a close as Eid approaches. The mood changes and the air is filled with a sense of anticipation and everyone gets ready for a grand celebration.

Spotting the Crescent Moon on Eid

The month of Ramadan lasts around twenty-eight days where people fast from sunrise to sunset.

The month ends on the twenty-ninth day with the festival of Eid. Children look forward to their new clothes, the festivities and the Eidie – a small amount of money they receive from the family's elders, and friends. The anticipation of the Big Day thus begins. People are impatient. Finally, the twenty-ninth day of Ramadan arrives.

On Eid, after breaking the fast, everyone rushes to an open field or a terrace and scans the horizon.

They are looking for the moon – a feeble, pale-yellow crescent. The moon is thin like a sickle or a curved dagger. The spotting of the moon means the month of Ramadan has ended. The fasting is over and the following day will be the first of Shawal – the tenth month of the Islamic calendar – when Eid al-Fitr will be celebrated.

THE TWO EIDS

Two Eids are celebrated across the globe – Eid al-Fitr and Eid al-Adha.

Eid al-Fitr

'Fitr' means breaking the fast. It heralds the end of Ramadan. It celebrates the conclusion of twenty-nine or thirty consecutive days of dawn-to-dusk fasting. It falls on the first of Shawwal, the tenth month of the Arabic calendar that follows Ramadan.

Eid al-Adha

It is more commonly known as 'Baqreed' across the Indian subcontinent. It marks the end of the annual Hajj pilgrimage in Mecca. There is a traditional symbolic sacrifice to renew the memory of the sacrifice made by Ibrahim, the founder of the Kaba, or the symbolic House of God in Mecca. The traditional word for sacrifice is 'Adha' derived from Arabic *udhiya*, meaning sacrifice.

Mentioned in the Quran, this day of spiritual purification and festivity is celebrated on the tenth day of the month of Dhul Hijj – the twelfth month of the Islamic calendar. It occurs less than two months after Eid al-Fitr.

How did Eid begin?

Tradition says that the festivals began after the Prophet Mohammad migrated to Medina, a city in western Saudi Arabia. The Prophet learnt that the locals had two annual festivals held on specific days since pre-Islamic days and were an occasion for fun. He replied by saying that Allah had given these festivals a better purpose and henceforth they were to be known as Eid al-Fitr and Eid al-Adha.

RAMADAN: PRAYERS, CHARITY, FASTING AND FEASTING

Eid al-Fitr cannot really be separated from Ramadan. The Ummah, or the Muslim community, gets ready for a month of fasting, abstinence, self-control and self-renewal. The *roza*, or fast, involves abstinence from any food or drink (including water) starting each day just before dawn and ending at dusk during the entire month of Ramadan.

Fasting

What the Quran says about fasting:

'Ye who believe! Fasting is prescribed to you . . . for a fixed number of days . . . And it is better for you that ye fast, if ye only knew . . . And glorify Him.'

Fasting, or more meaningfully abstinence, implies both physical restraint and self-control in thought and actions. Muslims are expected to exercise self-discipline, patience, humility, self-restraint and, most importantly, empathy for those around them who are not so fortunate, with the final aim of submission to the will of Allah. It makes them acutely conscious of the sufferings of fellow human beings. As a result of this prolonged fasting, they can appreciate the hunger and deprivation of those less fortunate and are also more prepared for the self-sacrifice to meet the needs of others.

Prayers

During the month, Muslims try to spend their maximum non-working time in prayers and remembrance of Allah. The setting Sun marks the end of the fast and the time for *Maghreb* prayers. The iftar, or breaking the fast, and *Maghreb* prayers are followed by *Ish'a*, or the night prayers, which would be followed by *Taraveeh*, the special congregational prayer of Ramadan in mosques.

Charity

Ramadan is considered blessed and Muslims often compete with each other to do good deeds. They try to emulate the Prophet by showing compassion and mercy. During Ramadan, those who successfully keep the fast, control their anger, don't use harsh words and bear with difficult people. They try to ignore and bear other's offenses as much as they can. This personal discipline is combined with charity.

Feasting

The iftar becomes an occasion in its own right. Families sit together and partake in this evening meal and big social gatherings with friends and family are organized around the iftar.

Households get busy with preparations of iftari – the foods consumed at iftar – from the afternoon. People get busy trying to think of food that would be most suitable after long fasting days.

People also use this occasion to arrange big community feasts. They invite friends and relatives for group iftars. Another common practice is to send the iftari to the local mosque for those who cannot afford it.

Some people even organize community meals for *suhoor* or *sehri* – the meal just before dawn to mark the start of the fast.

CELEBRATING EID IN INDIA

Eid Cuisine in India

Ramadan and Eid cuisine in India have a distinct local flavour to it. While it is customary to break the fast with dates irrespective of seasons or location, the food that follows as part of the iftar meal is based on local tastes.

During summers, delicious, energy-giving cold drinks and cooling foods are the order of the day. Kulfi with *falooda* and juices of seasonal fruits like *falsa* (blueberry), mango, cucumber, pineapple, orange and lemon are consumed. Fruits and salads of the season are cooled on ice and served. Specially prepared cold lentil dishes are other favourites. These are combined with vegetable preparations of cauliflower, spinach, onion, brinjal and samosas filled with either vegetables or minced meat.

During winters, the menus undergo a change. After dates and water, people like some hot soup, or *kahwa*, which is a kind of sweet Kashmiri tea, or *harira* (tomato and lentil soup) and sweetened milk with almonds. Deep-fried savouries and eggs feature in the winter menu and are served steaming hot. People also like to eat biryani, *sheermal* (a festive bread) and spicy korma.

On the Eid day, many special dishes are prepared. In fact, because of the emphasis on sweet dishes during this occasion, Eid al-Fitr, it is also called Meethi, or Sweet Eid. It is also known as Chhoti, or Smaller Eid, as against Eid al-Adha which is called Badi, or Bigger Eid.

Activities

1 GREET-AND-GROW EID CARD

Make a lovely little card that is so environment friendly you can plant it once the festival is over!

You Need:

• Different scraps of coloured paper • A blender or mixer • One packet seeds of any kind • Water • Three old towels • A piece of felt • One plain card (if you don't find this then you can make your own by folding some white chart paper) • Glue

Make It!

1) Put the scraps of paper along with water in the blender. Make sure it's not too watery but more like a thick shake.
2) Once it is well blended into a single coloured mush, gently mix in all the seeds (do not put in the mixer!) with a spoon.
3) Put the seed and paper mix onto the towel and let the excess water drain out.

4) Put a towel on a flat surface. Place the felt on top and put the mix in the centre. Cover with another towel and let it dry overnight.
5) When the mixture is dry and hard, cut out simple shapes like flowers, leaves or crescent moons and stick them with glue on your card.
6) Write 'Happy Eid' on the card and mention somewhere on it that the cut-out stuck on the card can be planted in a pot! Watch your card grow.

2 STAR AND MOON CURTAINS

This Eid, make a festive curtain for your room.

You Need:

• Different kinds of coloured paper or scraps from magazines and old cards • A pair of scissors • Needle and thick coloured thread • An old aluminium curtain rod

Make It!

1) Cut various phases of the moon (basically different parts of a circle) and stars from the paper.
2) String the needle with a long piece of thread and knot it at the end. Make a long chain of moons and stars. Leave a longish piece of thread free on top to tie around the curtain rod.
3) Make at least ten such chains.
4) Tie the ends of the moon and star chains around the rod.
5) Attach the rod to the pelmets of your door or window.

3 FANOOS LANTERN

Brighten up your Eid with a special lantern

You Need:

• Six pieces of A4 coloured square-shaped construction paper • Glue • A pair of scissors • Tape • Bright tassels • String to hang the lantern

Make It!

1) Fold each corner of a square paper into the centre. Now you will have a paper with four triangular-shaped flaps. Repeat this with the remaining five squares.
2) Using glue, attach each flap to another piece of square.
   Repeat until you have used up all the pieces of square paper that you folded earlier. Essentially, this is building a cube by using the corners of a square rather than the sides.
3) Attach the tassels. You can also use strips of construction paper.
4) Make a hole in one flap and thread the string to hang. You can also make a loop by twisting some wire.

4 EASY-PEASY EID TOFFEES

Carry them around in your pocket and gift a toffee to everyone you meet on Eid!

You Need:

• 500 gms icing sugar • 10 tbsp condensed milk • Few drops of food colouring • Few drops of flavouring (almond, peppermint, orange, etc.) • Two or three coloured cellophane sheets

Make It!

1) Mix the condensed milk and sugar into a stiff dough.
2) Break the dough into big balls.
3) Add the different food colours and flavouring into the separate balls.
4) Either flatten these out and use a cookie cutter to make shapes like stars and crescent moons, or simply roll into small round balls.
5) Keep inside the refrigerator for fifteen minutes to harden.
6) Cut the cellophane paper into little pieces and wrap the toffees in it, twisting the paper at either end.
7) Resist the temptation to eat them all at once.

5 STAINED-GLASS SADAQAH JAR

Collect coins in this jar through Ramadan and then give it to the needy or your local mosque on Eid day.

You Need:

• A glass or plastic jar • Acrylic paint • Fevicol or any other white glue • Paint brush • Palette

• Permanent black marker • Food colouring
• Dishwashing liquid

Make It!

1) Take your palette and add some glue, a few drops of dishwashing liquid and some food colour. Mix with your brush.
2) Clean your jar and paint the exterior with this homemade stained-glass paint.
3) Once dry, take the permanent black marker and draw stars, moons or the outline of a mosque. Colour in the details.
4) You can now collect your coins in this pretty jar. You only need to remember to fill it up by Eid.

6 DECORATIVE TILES

You Need:

• 1 plain square glazed tile • Glue • Ribbon
• Permanent markers • Acrylic paint • Varnish
• A pair of scissors

Make It!

1) Decide the length of the ribbon you want as a hanger for the tile.
2) Cut the ribbon and glue it, evenly spaced, on the back of the tile.
3) Let it dry and set.
4) Use permanent markers to draw directly on the tile.
5) Once the drawing is complete, paint it with acrylic colours.
6) Apply a coat of varnish and let it dry.
7) Hang the tile in your room. You can also leave out the ribbon and use the tile as a pretty tray for a bowl of dates.

7 EID BADGES

Decorate plain badges to make your very own colourful Eid button buddies to pin on your clothes on Eid.

You Need:

• A packet of plain plastic badges. Try and find as many colours as possible. If you cannot find plastic badges, buy a sheet of thick cardboard and two sheets of white chart-paper.

- Paints and paint brushes, or sketch-pens
- Strips of coloured paper for decoration
- Glue • A pair of scissors
- One packet of safety pins to attach the buttons to your clothes

Make It!

1) Make sure that all the badges are plain. Clean them if necessary.
2) In case you cannot find plastic badges, you can make some from thick cardboard. Cut out circles from a sheet of thick cardboard. Use glue to cover them with white chart paper on both sides. Make sure it is smooth on the surface.
3) Start with paints and sketch pens to draw on the buttons. Choose fun colours. You could draw stars and moons. Or even the mosque.
4) Write 'Eid Mubarak' along the sides of the badges.
5) You could further decorate the badges by using the strips of paper and sequins.
6) Carefully attach safety pins to each of the badges. You can also ask an adult to help you.
7) Attach the Eid badges onto your shirt or kurta.

MAHAVIR JAYANTI

Mahavir Jayanti is observed on the thirteenth day of the bright fortnight in Chaitra (March–April). It commemorates the birth of Lord Mahavira, the twenty-fourth and last Tirthankara or spiritual teacher of Jainism. It's a day that marks power of non-violence, compassion, and respect for all living beings.

Mahavira: The Prince Who Renounced Royalty and Adopted Ahimsa

According to Jain scriptures, Mahavira was born in the year 599 BCE in a royal family in India. However, at a young age, he was deeply troubled by the sufferings of people around him. Witnessing the struggles of animals and the inequalities of human society, a fire for change ignited within him. At the age of thirty, he renounced his royal life and embraced the path of a monk.

He endured twelve years of intense meditation and self-denial, conquering his own desires and embracing the principles of Ahimsa (non-violence) and Aparigraha (non-possession). He saw all living creatures as deserving of respect and protection. His teachings formed the fundamental beliefs of the Jain Dharma.

The Five Principles of Jainism

The five principles of Jainism offer a practical guide to achieving inner peace and harmony with all beings. Ahimsa tells us to treat every living being non-violently. Aparigraha, non-possessiveness, urges us to let go of attachment to material things and cultivate contentment. Satya, truthfulness, emphasizes living with integrity and transparency. Brahmacharya, celibacy, encourages self-control and good conduct. Anekantavada says that we should be open to different viewpoints. These five principles show us the path to self-realization and pave the way for a life of compassion, non-violence, and spiritual enlightenment.

The Significance of Mahavir Jayanti

Mahavir Jayanti isn't just about celebrating the birth of a great guru; it's about celebrating the ideals he championed. It's a day to reaffirm commitment to Ahimsa, to extend compassion to all living beings, and to strive for a world free from violence and suffering.

How Jains Observe the Festival

On Mahavir Jayanti, temples are adorned with vibrant flowers. Hymns and prayers are also chanted. Young and old gather, dressed in their finest clothes, to pay their respects to Lord Mahavira. They organize ahimsa rallies, marching through streets with placards, spreading the message of non-violence and kindness. Bird feeders are hung in gardens. The day is marked by acts of charity and service, as Jains donate food to the needy and offer shelter to stray animals.

Across India and the world, Mahavir Jayanti bursts into life with vibrant hues and diverse traditions in various Jain temples. At Sonagiri in Gujarat, the festival unfolds with a unique Mahamastakabhisheka, an anointing ceremony. The Dilwara Temples in Rajasthan resonate with hymns and rangoli patterns. Each temple celebrates Mahavir Jayanti in a way that reflects its unique heritage and strengthens the community's bond with Lord Mahavira's timeless teachings.

The spirit of Mahavir Jayanti extends far beyond the confines of temples and rituals. Jains strive to live by his principles in their daily lives. They practice vegetarianism, speak with truth and kindness and avoid unnecessary harm to any living being. They walk barefoot on Earth so that they do not tread on any creature.

Mahavira's teachings show us how to build a more compassionate and sustainable future.

ACTIVITIES

1 JAIN SWASTIKA

Ask your parents if you can draw a Jain swastika on the outer wall of your home's entrance or designated worshipping space.

You Need:

- *Kumkum* (vermillion) in a bowl
- Water

Make It!

1) Wet the *kumkum* with a few drops of water.
2) Draw an equal-armed cross on your chosen surface using your ring finger as a paintbrush.
3) Draw four straight lines at 45° angles, one line for every arm of the cross. The lines should extend in a clockwork direction.
4) Then, draw three dots horizontally above the swastika.
5) Above that, make a half-moon or crescent shape with its curve pointing downwards.

6) Add a single dot in the centre above the moon.

Every detail represents a unique aspect of Jainism. Jains associate the four arms of a holy swastika with the four states of existence. The three dots represent a straight path to enlightenment. The crescent stands for a perfect state of liberation.

2 FILL IN THE COLOURS

The flag of Jainism has five colours: white, red, yellow, green and blue. They represent the religion's five vows.

Create an image of your choice and use only the five colours mentioned above.

3 UNSCRAMBLE MAHAVIRA'S TEACHINGS

Given below are the five main teachings of Lord Mahavira. The alphabets are all present but their arrangement looks off. See if you can figure out what Lord Mahavira wished to teach us.

1) aismha (non-violence) ________________

2) asyat (truth) ________________

3) taesya (non-stealing) ________________

4) rayhmbacarah (chastity) ________________

5) rpgariaaha (non-attachment to things) ________________

4 HEALTHY SNACK JAYANTI

Help your family expand their list of vegan snacks with these simple recipes. Adjust the ingredients as per the number of people.

Kela Vada

You Need:

• 2 large semi-raw bananas • 2 chopped green chillies • Mango powder
• 150–200 gms gram flour (besan) • 50 gms rice flour
• Tamarind pulp • Sugar • Cooking oil • Salt
• Other spices

Make It!

1) Mix sugar and a pinch of salt with the tamarind pulp to make tamarind chutney.
2) Peel and mash the bananas.
3) Add all the spices to the mashed bananas. Don't forget the green chillies!
4) Using your hands, roll the mash into small balls.

5) Prepare a batter with the two kinds of flour and water. Add a pinch of red chilli powder for taste. If your spice tolerance is low, you can do without it.
6) Ask an adult to cover the banana balls with batter and deep-fry them.
7) Serve with chutney and enjoy.

Black Chickpea Chaat

You Need:

• 1 cup boiled black chickpea (*kala chana*) • Chopped green and red bell pepper • Red chilli powder • Chaat masala • Dry mango powder • Chopped spinach leaves • Chopped cabbage • Cooking oil • Salt

Make It!

1) Ask an adult to medium-fry ½ cups each of green bell pepper and cabbage in one teaspoon of oil.
2) Add ½ a cup of red bell pepper, followed by black chickpea, salt and other spices.
3) You may also squeeze half a lemon for added taste.
4) Add spinach leaves and cook for less than five minutes on low heat.
5) Ask your parents or siblings to taste your black chickpea chaat.

Answers:

1) ahimsa, 2) satya, 3) asteya, 4) brahmacharya, 5) aparigraha

BUDDHA PURNIMA

Buddha Purnima celebrates the birth of Gautama Buddha, the founder of Buddhism. It comes around in the month of Vaisakha (April–May) and is also known as Vaisakhi Purnima. The festival commemorates the milestones of the Buddha's enlightenment and *Parinirvana* or final liberation. It marks a journey that illuminates the path to liberation from suffering for all who seek it.

The Journey of Siddhartha Gautama

Siddhartha Gautama was born into a royal family in the ancient Indian city of Lumbini, now in Nepal. He lived in a palace. Even though he had everything he wanted, he felt sad thinking about how life is not always happy and that everyone goes through difficult times like getting old, being sick, and eventually passing away. So, at the age of twenty-nine, he decided to give up the comfort of his princely life and go on a journey to understand the world.

For six years, Siddhartha lived a simple and tough life. He put his body and mind through extreme challenges.

Yet, he couldn't find peace. Finally, under a Bodhi tree in Bodh Gaya, in present-day Bihar, he meditated deeply to understand important things about life. In that silence, he came face to face with the harshness of life and fought the power of desire. He ultimately attained enlightenment, and learnt the 'Four Noble Truths' and the 'Eightfold Path,' the practical map to help reach the ultimate goal.

The Four Noble Truths and the Eightfold Path

These truths weren't mere philosophical ideas; they were a call to action. These truths illuminated the path from the darkness of suffering to the gentle dawn of liberation. The Eightfold Path has eight spokes: right view, right intention, right speech, right action, right livelihood, right effort, right mindfulness and right concentration. They provided a practical framework for this journey to reach the Four Noble Truths. The Buddha realized that life was about becoming more aware and compassionate. And that a good human being should align their thoughts, words and actions with the principles of non-violence, truthfulness and generosity.

This is how Buddha Purnima becomes more than a celebration. It becomes a festival of hope and transformation. It reminds us that everyone can seek and gain enlightenment. That all of us can live a life of kindness and compassion and end the suffering of others.

Buddha Purnima Traditions and Rituals

Across the globe, Buddhist communities infuse their own cultural traditions in their celebration of Buddha Purnima. In Bodh Gaya, pilgrims offer prayers, join processions and light lamps. In Southeast Asia, lanterns carrying wishes and prayers take flight on rivers. In Tibet, artists set up monumental butter sculptures of Buddha. And in temples around the world, the story of the Buddha's wisdom is shared with devotees and communities gather in shared joy.

Embracing the Buddha's Message in Daily Life

Buddha Purnima is not just about rituals. It invites all of us to embrace the Buddha's message in our day-to-day life. It is about paying attention to our thoughts and emotions without judgment. It's about being compassionate and kind – not just to others but also to ourselves. His lessons teach us to let go and not hold on to our wants and desires. They tell us to always speak the truth and use our words to uplift and inspire others. Adopting the principles of non-violence, honesty and generosity on Buddha Purnima and the rest of the year makes the world a kinder place.

ACTIVITIES

1 MAKE A BUDDHA PORTRAIT

Create a portrait of Lord Buddha without the hassle of details.

You Need:

- A sheet of paper • Pencil
- Crayons or pencil colours

Make It!

1) Trace an outline of the Buddha sitting with his knees crossed.
2) Don't draw any details inside the frame. Make a small bun on the top of his head.
3) Fill this image with black colour. This is called a silhouette.
4) Make a large circle behind the Buddha to represent the sun.
5) Fill this part of the image with the right colours.
6) Similarly, you can also draw a tree behind the Buddha to denote the Bodhi tree.

2 PRACTISE MINDFULNESS WITH BUDDHA

Not all festivals are about splendour and pomp. This Buddha Purnima, learn how to meditate like the Buddha.

You Need:

- Yoga mat or a clean surface to sit on
- Silence

Do It!

1) Sit down with your legs crossed and your palms on your knees.
2) Close your eyes.
3) Pay attention to the movement of your stomach as you breathe in and out slowly.
4) Listen to your breathing.
5) Listen to the subtle sounds around you. It could be the ticking of a wall clock or the chirping of a bird outside.
6) The point is to be present and forget your thoughts for a few moments.

3 PRACTISE THE EIGHTFOLD RESOLUTIONS

Buddha's eightfold path is a crucial teaching of Buddhism. It includes practising the right understanding, thought, speech, action, livelihood, effort, mindfulness and concentration.

Sit with your parents, grandparents or elder siblings and figure out ways in which you can follow the eightfold path in the best way possible. Note down your goals below:

____

____

____

____

____

____

____

____

4 SET UP A FOOD STAND

There are numerous ways to practise compassion. A food stand could be one of them.

You Need:

• A large table • Leaf bowls • Rubber bands

Do It!

1) Pick a day that suits you.
2) You can set up a food stand in front of your building or your front yard, if your house has one.

Otherwise, you can ask your local authorities for a day's permission to set it up in a local park.

3) Request an adult to prepare rice *kheer*.
4) Store it in big, well-packed containers so it doesn't spoil in the heat.
5) Put up a sign to inform passers-by of your *kheer* stand.
6) Ask your neighbourhood friends to help you with distributing the *kheer*.
7) Before giving the *kheer* away, use two or more leaf bowls and a rubber band to package it properly.

5 TEST YOUR BUDDHA KNOWLEDGE

Fill in the blank spaces to see how much you have learnt.

1) The Buddha was born here ____UM____I____I
2) This was Buddha's clan name G____UT____ ____A
3) The Buddha attained enlightenment here BO____H ____AY____
4) This marks a release from *samskara* (cycle of rebirth) NI____V____ ____A

Answers: 1) Lumbini, 2) Gautama, 3) Bodh Gaya, 4) Nirvana

RATH YATRA

Every year in mid-summer, Lord Jagannath, with his elder brother Balabhadra and sister Subhadra, goes on vacation, travelling on chariots, from his temple in Puri to his garden palace in the countryside. This belief has given rise to one of the biggest religious festivals in India – the Rath Yatra.

Jagannath, believed to be an avatar of Lord Vishnu, is the Lord of Puri – the coastal town of Odisha. Rath Yatra is of great significance to the people of Odisha. It is during this time that the three deities of Jagannath, Balabhadra and Subhadra are taken out in a grand procession in specially made gigantic temple-like chariots called raths, which are pulled by thousands of devotees.

Historical Origin

Many believe that the custom of placing idols on grand chariots and pulling them is of Buddhist origin. Fa Hien, the Chinese historian, who visited India in the fifth century AD, had written about the chariot of Buddha being pulled along public roads.

The Origin of 'Juggernaut'

History has it that when the British first observed the Rath Yatra in the eighteenth century, they were so amazed that they sent home shocking descriptions. This gave rise to the term 'juggernaut', meaning 'destructive force'. This connotation may have originated from the occasional but accidental death of some devotees under the chariot wheels caused by the crowd and commotion.

How the Festival Is Celebrated

The festival begins with the Ratha Prathistha or invoking ceremony in the morning, but the Ratha Tana, or chariot pulling, is the most exciting part of the festival, which begins in the late afternoon when the chariots of Jagannath, Balabhadra and Subhadra start rolling. Each of these carriages have different specifications: The chariot of Lord Jagannath is called Nandighosa, has eighteen wheels and is 45 feet high. The chariot of Balabhadra called Taladhvaja has sixteen wheels and is 44 feet high. Devadalana, the chariot of Subhadra, has fourteen wheels and is 43 feet high.

Each year these wooden chariots are constructed anew in accordance with religious specifications. The idols of these three deities are also made of wood and they are replaced by new ones every twelve years. After a nine-day sojourn of the deities at the country temple, the divine summer vacation gets over and the three return to the city temple of Lord Jagannath.

The Puri Rath Yatra is world famous for the crowd that it attracts. Puri plays host to devotees, tourists and about ten lakh pilgrims.

Fourteen tailors are engaged in stitching up the chariots' covers that require almost 1,200 meters of cloth. Orissa's government-run textile mill usually supply the cloth needed to decorate the chariots. However, other Mumbai-based mills also donate cloth for the Rath Yatra.

ACTIVITIES

1 HOLY MALPUA

Help your family prepare this traditional sweet dish eaten during Lord Jagannath's festival.

You Need:

• Banana • Milk • Wheat flour • Chopped almonds • Sugar • Cardamom and cardamom powder • Cream • Saffron food colouring • *Suji* (semolina)

Make It!

1) Blend a banana and ½ cup of milk.
2) Add a cup of wheat flour, a little *suji*, cardamom powder and cream to this blend.
3) As you start mixing it, keep adding some more milk. Let an adult help you with determining the quantities required.
4) Whisk it for a few minutes and then let it rest.
5) Prepare a sugar syrup with sugar, water and three to four pods of cardamom. The sugar needs to melt completely.

6) Let an adult cook the syrup for five minutes.
7) Add a pinch of food colouring to it.
8) An adult now needs to fry the malpua batter and dip it in sugar syrup.
9) Once the malpuas are ready, you can garnish them with chopped nuts.

2 CLEANSING RITUALS

Every important day begins with a good cleanse.

You Need:

- Idols or figurines of Jagannath, Baladev and Subhadhra
- A large tray
- Rose petals
- Clean cloth

Do It!

1) Use a tray that can hold a good amount of water.
2) Sprinkle rose petals on the water.
3) Place the three idols in the tray, Jagannath in the middle and the other two beside him.
4) Take some rose water in your palm and gently wash the idols.
5) Once done, take the idols out of the water and dry them with a clean cloth.

3 2-D CHARIOT

There is no Yatra without a Ratha! Design a chariot you would want to be part of the procession or use the one given.

Start with large wheels and a platform to install the idol, which a temple-like structure will then protect. Use different colours of your choice. Feel free to add any other details that you can think of.

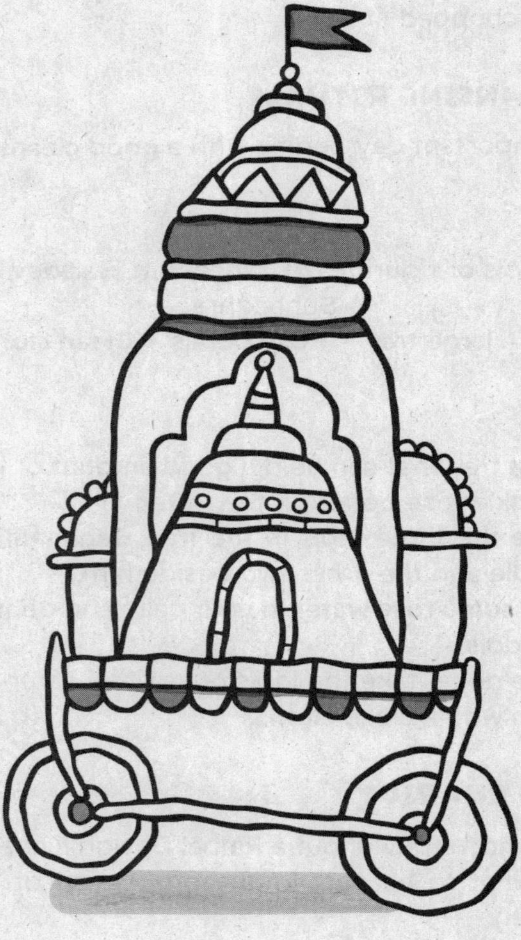

4 CONNECT THE DOTS

Complete the sentences below.

1) During Rath Yatra, Lord ___________, Balabhadra and ___________ are taken out in a grand procession.

2) People pull the ___________ of Lord Jagannath during the procession.

3) Ratha Tana means ______________________.

4) The chariots are made from ______________.

5) One of the famous locations for Rath Yatra celebrations in India is __________.

6) The word juggernaut means __________________.

5 WHAT'S IN A NAME?

The jumble of letters below hides within them the names of the procession's three main chariots. Can you find them?

N	T	J	I	C	W	J	R	C	N	J
X	A	H	S	F	V	M	I	W	D	H
D	L	N	O	N	Y	V	L	P	B	D
Q	A	O	D	G	K	P	Q	E	R	L
T	D	P	M	I	D	G	M	C	Z	U
N	H	J	L	Z	G	W	A	Q	C	B
V	V	Z	E	R	F	H	Y	I	L	J
S	A	A	Q	F	B	C	O	C	D	T
H	J	R	N	A	T	A	L	S	A	F
L	A	W	E	R	M	I	P	P	H	T
F	D	E	V	A	D	A	L	A	N	A

Answers:
1) Jagannath, Subhadra, 2) Rath or Chariot, 3) Chariot pulling, 4) Wood, 5) Puri, 6) Destructive force

RAKHI

Rakshabandhan, or Rakhi, is a special day in the Hindu calendar. It falls on full-moon day in the month of Shravan. It is a day to celebrate the special bond between brothers and sisters. Sisters tie a sacred thread called *rakhi* on their brothers' right hand.

Bounds and Protects

Rakshabandhan means 'a bond of protection'. A sister prays for the long life of her brother. And in return, the brother vows to forever protect the sister. *Rakhi*s are ideally made of silk with gold and silver threads, beautifully crafted embroidered sequins and studded with semi-precious stones. But nowadays, they come in all kinds of designs.

A *rakhi* may not always be shared just between a brother and sister. In fact, when a *rakhi* is tied on the wrists of close friends and neighbours, it also signifies a bond of protection and a life of peace and co-existence. Festivals like Rakhi have always helped ease tensions between siblings, families and communities in India.

The Auspicious Full Moon

In Northern India, the full moon night of Rakshabandhan or Rakhi Purnima is also called Kajri Purnima or Kajri Navami. That is when wheat or barley is sown and goddess Bhagwati is worshipped. In Western Indian states, the festival is called Nariyal Purnima or the Coconut Full Moon. In Southern India, it is known as Shravan Purnima, which is an important religious occasion.

RAKHI IN HINDU MYTHOLOGY

Hindu mythology, including the Puranas, the Ramayana and the Mahabharata, speak of the *rakhi* as a bonding power. It also symbolizes all aspects of protection of good from evil forces.

Varuna and Rakhi

Rakhi was originally meant to be a ritual offering for the sea-god Lord Varuna, according to one mythological tale. So, devotees offer coconuts and flowers to Varuna. Ceremonial bathing and fairs at waterfronts are held on the day of Rakshabandhan. This tradition of worshipping Varuna during the Rakhi festival is popular, especially in Western India.

Indra and Rakhi

According to another mythological legend, when Lord Indra, the King of the Heavens, was unable to cope with the constant attacks waged by Daitya Raja, the Demon King, he sought the advice of Devaguru Brihaspati, the Guru of the Gods. Upon Brihaspati's advice, Indra's wife Indrani tied a *rakhi* on Indra's wrist on Shravan Purnima. It is said that the *rakhi* gave Indra the power to vanquish the Demon King. Thus, the sacred silken thread helped Indra regain control over his heavenly empire.

Yama and Rakhi

Even Yama, the Lord of Death, is said to have observed Rakshabandhan. His sister Yamuna had tied the *rakhi* on Yama's wrist during prayers and rituals. Deeply touched by his sister's love, Yama granted her immortality. So, it is believed that a *rakhi* tied by a sister on the day of Rakshabandhan can protect a brother from sudden death.

Yudhishthira and Rakhi

In the Mahabharata, Lord Krishna advises King Yudhishthira, the eldest of the Pandava brothers, to tie a *rakhi* to to protect himself from the perils of the great war of Kurukshetra. Yudhisthira is said to have observed the ceremony of Rakshabandhan and tied the sacred thread around his own wrist. Stories from the Mahabharata also mention Kunti, the mother of the Pandavas, tying a *rakhi* on her grandson Abhimanyu's wrist. It is also said that Draupadi, the wife of the

Pandavas, observed Rakshabandhan by presenting the *rakhi* to Lord Krishna.

Bali, Vishnu, Lakshmi and Rakhi

In the mythological tales from the *Puranas,* we find the beautiful legend of Bali, the grandson of Vishnu devotee Prahalada. Lord Vishnu was so impressed by the might of Bali that he promised him divine protection and immortality until Bali was crowned King. As the legend goes, Vishnu left Vaikunth, his abode in the heavens, and started guarding Bali's kingdom. Vishnu's wife, Lakshmi, was alarmed at her husband's action and decided to bring the Lord back to heaven. Lakshmi disguised herself as a Brahmin woman and went to Bali to seek protection till her husband returned. He welcomed her into his palace. As Shravana Purnima dawned, Lakshmi tied a *rakhi* on Bali's wrist. Bali was greatly touched by this gesture and asked her what she wanted as a gift. Lakshmi then revealed her real identity and asked Bali to let go of her husband Vishnu. Bali promised to keep his words on the condition that the couple should visit his palace every year on Rakshabandhan.

Since then, people say that brothers invite sisters to their home on Shravan Purnima to celebrate the occasion with a feast. Hence, Rakshabandhan is also called 'Baleva' after King Bali's legendary devotion.

ACTIVITIES

1 MAKE YOUR OWN RAKHI

Here's a step-by-step guide to help you make a traditional *rakhi* this Rakshabandhan.

You Need:

• Strands of silk threads • A pair of scissors • Cotton thread to tie knots • Beads, sitaras, golden threads and sponges to decorate • Glue • A toothbrush with hard bristles

Make It!

1) Take 24-inch silk thread strands in a bunch. If you want to make multi-coloured *rakhis*, take silk threads of different colours.
2) Tie a tight knot with a cotton thread at about the one-fourth mark of the silken thread bunch. This part will be made into a *rakhi* while three-fourths will be the string to tie around the wrist.

3) Make sure the heads of the silk threads of the one fourth part of the bunch are not in loops. In case they are, cut them with a pair of scissors.
4) Once they are free of loops, rub these threads hard with a toothbrush using strong strokes by holding on to the knot tightly. With repeated strokes, the silk threads will turn fluffy and soft.

5) To make the string, divide the three-fourth part of the silk thread in two equal parts and plait them separately. If you are unable to plait, ask an adult for help. At the end, tie a knot and brush again.
6) Once this is done, decorate it with beads or *sitara*s. Stick them on with glue.

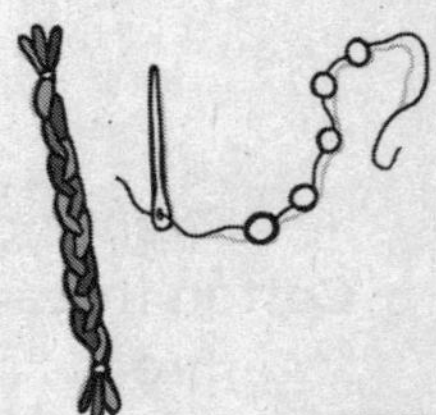

7) You can also buy a sheet of sponge of a suitable colour, cut it into a star or flower shape and decorate it with beads. Golden threads can be woven together and used for decoration.

2 STRING RAKHI

A simple *rakhi* that is a breeze to make!

You Need:

• Notebook or clipboard (use any flat surface) • Three strands of different-coloured string • Masking tape (use this to tape your rakhi down)

Make It!

1) Match your strands of string according to their colour.
2) Make sure your bracelet is long enough. Measure from the tip of your fingers to your shoulder, then double it.
3) Fold the measured string in half, exactly in the middle.
4) With the fold intact, form a loop at the centre of the threads.
5) Tie a knot at the bottom of the loop, leaving it approximately one-inch long.
6) Attach the loop under the clip of the clipboard or tape it to a notebook.
7) Separate the threads in an alternating colour pattern. Using your first string, tie a knot around each of the remaining five strings in order. Your first string is now at the end of the six strings.
8) Repeat with each of the remaining five strings. You should be able to see the pattern emerging at this point.
9) Continue to tie knots until you're left with a couple of inches of unknotted thread.
10) On Rakhi day, tie the unknotted thread around your brother's hand!

3 POCKET WALL HANGING

A perfect gift for Rakhi because who doesn't need an extra pocket or two? Make sure an adult helps you with the handling of needles and scissors.

You Need:

• Colourful waste cloths • Needle and thread • A pair of scissors

Make It!

1) Cut out a rectangle the size you want your wall hanging to be out of the cloth.
2) Decide on the pocket size. Cut pockets out of the leftover fabric. If you are feeling lazy, go ahead and cut out the pockets of an old pair of jeans.
3) Pin them where you want them on the large rectangle. Sew on three sides, with the top of each pocket left open.
4) Sew a piece on the hanging or stick it to the wall with double-sided tape.
5) Your sibling's Pocket Wall Hanging is ready! Fill pockets with supplies, like their favourite pens, keys, etc.

4 PICK-UP STICKS

A traditional Chinese game for hours of sibling fun!

You Need:

• Paints and paintbrushes • Thirty thin wooden sticks (you can replace them with plastic straws, but being lighter, the game is much tougher)

Make It!

1) To make your set of pick-up sticks, paint the ends of your thirty wooden sticks with the following

colours: one black, three red, five blue, nine green and twelve yellow.

2) Assign points to each colour as follows: black - ten points, red - five points, blue - three points, green - two points and yellow - one point.
3) Use a table or the floor to play the game. Hold the sticks upright in a bunch in one hand just above the floor or table. Release the sticks and let them fall. Now try to remove the sticks one by one without moving any other stick in the pile.
4) You can use the black stick to help you remove other sticks. Now, taking turns, remove sticks from the pile until you move another by mistake.
5) Once a mistake is made, count the value of your sticks. Keep playing - the first to get to a hundred points is the winner!

5 IT'S A LINE-UP

A Tic-Tac-Toe variant that will save you from hours of boredom.

You Need:

• Paper • Pencils • Two or more players

Play It!

1) Draw a table with forty-two squares, seven across and six down.
2) The game starts from the bottom of the grid, upwards.

3) The winner is the first to make a horizontal, vertical or diagonal row of four. All other rules remain the same as the traditional Tic-Tac-Toe.

6 STRING PICTURES

A beautiful gift for Rakhi to bring a smile to your sibling's face!

You Need:

• Stiff card • Pencil • Thin brush • Coloured strings of wool • Soft cloth

Make It!

1) Cut a piece of card paper.
2) Lightly sketch out a picture with the pencil. Draw only the outlines — trees, flowers, animals.
3) Brush glue over the pencil lines.
4) Now stick on the strings of wool neatly over glue marks.
5) Press down firmly with a cloth.
6) Hang up your picture if you like or make a card with it.

KRISHNA JANMASHTAMI

Krishna was born at midnight on the *ashtami* or the eighth day of the dark fortnight in the Hindu month of Shravan (August–September). This day is called Janmashtami. Scholars have now accepted the period between 3200 and 3100 BCE as the period in which Lord Krishna lived on Earth.

Krishna was a mischievous child who loved music and pranks. As an adult, Krishna drove the chariot of the warrior Arjuna, whose story is chronicled in the Bhagavad Gita.

Janmashtami celebrations

On the eve of Janmashtami, devotees fast for the whole day and night. They recite hymns from the Gita, sing devotional songs, and chant the mantra *Om namo Bhagavate Vasudevaya*. Dances and dramatic reenactments of the Janmashtami myths are performed during the day.

At midnight, the fast ends, and the Krishna statues are bathed in milk and honey, or in water that has been treated with a combination of spices: cloves, cardamom, saffron, Tulasi and rose petals.

On the second day, (Janam Ashtami), the Chappan Bhog is collected, a huge offering of fifty-six of Krishna's favourite foods. Those include cereals, dried and fresh fruits, sweets, pickles, and nuts; each of the fifty-six must include a quantity of eight. After the offering, the foods are distributed to the participants. Iin some of the larger cities, the Dahi Handi is performed. Clay pots containing butter, curd, and money are strung high up on buildings, and young men form human pyramids to compete with one another to break the pots.

Story of the Birth of Lord Krishna

According to stories recorded at least as long ago as the fifth century CE, Krishna was born in Mathura, the son of Devaki, the beloved sister of King Kamsa, who had arranged her marriage to Vasudeva. At the wedding, a voice came from the heavens and told Kamsa that he would be killed by the eighth son of Devaki and Vasudeva. In fear, Kamsa threw the couple into a prison and vowed to kill all their children.

Kamsa killed the first six of their children. Miraculously, the seventh son, Balram, was transferred from Devaki's womb to that of Princess Rohini in Vrindavan, where he stayed alive.

Devaki's eighth baby was incarnated as Vishnu in the womb. And when he was born, the guards fell asleep and the doors of the jail magically opened. Vasudeva smuggled Krishna out of the prison to his friend Nanda.

A frightening thunderstorm and heavy rainfall made the trip difficult, but Shesh Nag, the snake god, sheltered them from the storm.

Vasudeva gave Krishna to Nanda and his wife Yashoda and took their daughter. He carried the girl child and went back to prison. The doors locked behind him, the guards awoke and went to tell Kamsa that a girl had been born, not a boy. Kamsa rushed to the jail and attempted to dash the baby to her death. But the baby rose into the sky and took the form of the Goddess Durga, warning Kamsa about how his death would occur.

Krishna grew up in Gokul and returned to Mathura, freed his parents and killed Kamsa as had been foretold.

ACTIVITIES

1 DRESSMAKER OF VRINDAVAN

Style a garment for Laddu Gopal for a quick Janmasthami dress-up.

You Need:

• A piece of fabric • A pair of scissors • Glue or a sewing kit • Silver or golden lace

Make It!

1) From a fabric of your choice, neatly cut out a circular piece. Keep in mind the size of your Laddu Gopal figurine.
2) Fold the circle in half and then half again. Cut a little part off the tapering triangular edge.
3) Open the circle up. Use glue to attach lace to its outer and inner rims.
4) Ask an adult to help you use a needle and thread to sew the lace onto the cloth.
5) Your Laddu Gopal's new outfit is ready to be put on!

2 SAFE JANMASHTAMI

Enjoy Janmashtami to the fullest while keeping your environment safe.

Dos and Don'ts of Janmashtami Decor

1) Use old figurines for your Janmashtami tableau instead of buying new ones every year.
2) Use dupattas and newspaper decorations instead of materials you cannot reuse later.
3) Fresh flowers, instead of plastic and artificial ones, add life to the celebration.
4) Talk to your parents and consider using plates made out of leaves to serve prasad.

3 DAHI HANDI WITH A TWIST

While the traditional game of Dahi Handi is not for everyone to play, you can always add a twist to let maximum people take part in it.

You Need:

- Several small metal pots or steel glasses
- *Dahi* (curd)

Play It!

1) A chosen referee can hide many pots of *dahi* in different parts of the house.
2) Players can divide themselves into teams and set off to find as many pots as they can.

3) The team whose members find the most number of pots wins.

4 FLOWER PETAL NECKLACE

Make a tiny garland for Laddu Gopal.

You Need:

- Sewing kit • Petals of different sizes and colours

Make It!

1) Insert a white thread into a sewing needle. Let an adult supervise you during this step.
2) Knot the free end of your thread. However, leave two centimetres of thread before the knot so it can be easily tied up later.
3) Take a petal and pierce its centre with the needle.
4) Begin sliding the petals through the needle and onto the thread.
5) When the thread has enough petals, cut the needle off.
6) Tie the two ends together to complete the garland.
7) Place it around your figurine's neck.

5 TELL STORIES WITH TAMBOLA

Learn about Krishna's dramatic childhood through the rules of Tambola.

You Need:

- Small square sheets of paper • Pens • Ruler

Play It!

1) On a square sheet, make a grid of six squares with the help of a ruler.
2) Every square will contain the keywords of any one of Krishna's popular childhood legends. Some of the legends are: Krishna's birth, Krishna and the demon Arishtasura, Krishna and the serpent Kaaliya, the universe in Krishna's mouth, *Maakhan chor*, Govardhan hill, the forest fire, and the naming of Govinda.
3) Ask your elders or refer to the web for more such stories and write them down.
4) Do the same with every square sheet, with a different mix of stories on every sheet.
5) Distribute the sheets amongst your cousins and friends.
6) A chosen referee will call out the name of a story and the person who gets that story in their card will cross it out.
7) Anyone who crosses all of their stories out wins the game.
8) The group will then recount the stories on the winner's cards.

GANESH CHATURTHI

As the god of beginnings, Ganesha is celebrated at events big and small. The biggest of them is Ganesh Chaturthi, the great Ganesha festival. It is celebrated by people around the world as the birthday of Lord Ganesha. It is observed during the Hindu month of Bhadra (mid-August to mid-September). and the grandest and most elaborate of them, especially in the western India state of Maharashtra, lasts for ten days, ending on the day of 'Ananta Chaturdashi'.

How Ganesha Was Born

The most common story of Ganesha's birth is depicted in the Hindu scripture Shiva Purana. In this epic, the goddess Parvati creates a boy from the dirt she has washed off her body. She assigns him the task of guarding the entrance to her bathroom. When her husband Shiva returns, he is surprised to find the strange boy denying him access. In a rage, Shiva decapitates him.

Parvati breaks down in grief. To soothe her, Shiva sends out his warriors to fetch the head of any sleeping being who is found facing the north. They return with the severed head of an elephant, which is attached to the boy's body. Shiva revives the boy, making him the leader of his troops. Shiva also ordains that people will worship Ganesha and invoke his name before undertaking any venture.

The Grand Celebration

For Ganesh Chaturthi, a life-like clay model of Lord Ganesha is made. The size of this idol may vary from 3/4th of an inch to over 25 feet.

On the day of the festival, it is placed on raised platforms in homes or in outdoor tents for people to pay their homage. The priest then invokes life into the idol amidst the chanting of mantras. This ritual is called *pranapratishhtha*. After this, the sixteen ways of paying tribute follow. Coconut, jaggery, twenty-one *modaks* (rice flour preparation), twenty-one *durva* (trefoil) blades and red flowers are offered.

For ten days, from Bhadrapad Shudh Chaturthi to the Ananta Chaturdashi, Ganesha is worshiped. On the eleventh day, the idol is taken through the streets in a procession accompanied by dancing, singing, to be immersed in a river or the sea. This symbolizes a ritual see-off of the Lord in his journey towards his abode in Kailash while taking away with him the misfortunes of all mankind. All join in this final procession, shouting 'Ganapathi Bappa Morya, Purchya Varshi Laukariya' (O father Ganesha, come again early next year).

The whole community comes to worship Ganesha in beautifully done tents. These also serve as the venue for free medical check-ups, blood donation camps, a charity for the poor, dramatic performances, films, devotional songs, etc. during the days of the festival.

Include an oval here or use a cute font which says:

Colour me!

ACTIVITIES

1 PEEPAL GANESHA

Make your own Ganesha.

You Need:

- Eight *peepal* leaves (make sure one of them has a longer tip than others)
- A surface you want Ganesha on (newspaper sheet, cardboard, etc.)
- Glue

Make It!

1) Keep the single leaf with a longer tip aside for now. We will call this the head.
2) Take the biggest leaf from the lot and keep it on your surface. Its tip should point upwards. We will call this the body.
3) Take two leaves and tuck them beneath the lower left and right halves of the body.

4) Position them in a way that they look like folded knees.
5) Take two more leaves and tuck them above the knees on both sides. They should look like the palms of Ganesha's hands.
6) Place the head above the body. Its tip should point towards Ganesha's left palm.
7) Tuck the remaining two leaves behind Ganesha's head on both sides to make his ears.
8) Glue the leaves on a surface of your choice. Make sure you don't spoil a wall!

2 LEARN WITH PUPPETS

Narrate and learn stories with the help of DIY Ganesh Chaturthi puppets.

You Need:

- Ice cream sticks
- Handmade or card stock paper sheets
- Glue
- Friends and family

Make It!

1) Refer to the stories you have learnt about Lord Ganesha and draw their major characters on multi-coloured sheets of paper.
2) For deities or characters whose faces are complicated to represent, you may choose symbols that are central to their attire. For instance, Lord Shiva can be represented by his trident.

3) Cut these miniature drawings out.
4) Use glue to stick them on separate ice cream sticks.
5) You can now assemble your friends or family and act out Ganesha's stories with the help of these puppets.

3 WORD SEARCH

Of the 108 names of Lord Ganesha, a few are hiding in this jumble of letters below. Find the following words: Vignaharta, Heramba, Gajanana, Kapila, Mahodara and Purush.

M	D	T	W	V	A	S	Q	F	B
P	U	E	Q	F	B	N	E	Y	M
V	S	G	Y	E	J	S	N	U	E
W	I	H	E	R	A	M	B	A	N
R	W	G	H	S	X	A	N	H	Y
D	J	A	N	K	L	H	B	X	S
T	U	J	K	A	X	O	Q	R	N
C	Z	A	U	P	H	D	P	W	S
M	U	N	C	I	T	A	U	Y	U
W	G	A	J	L	D	R	R	A	K
L	P	N	Q	A	X	A	U	T	D
T	K	A	G	J	C	Z	S	T	A
H	D	K	B	C	W	U	H	I	P

4 TEST YOUR GANPATI KNOWLEDGE

Match the words in Column A to those in Column B.

Column A	Column B
1. Ganesha's ride	a. Modak
2. Another name for Parvati	b. Ganeshotsav
3. Another name for Ganesh Chaturthi	c. Kartikeya
4. Festival's ritual food offering	d. Mushak
5. Ganesha's younger brother	e. Uma

5 STICKY MODAK FINGERS

Sweets can't melt in your mouth unless you make them!

You Need:

• Sweet stuffing • Rice flour dough
• A large plate or tray

Make It!

1) Request an adult to prepare the stuffing and dough beforehand. Help them with it if you can.
2) Once the dough is ready, break and shape it into small, smooth balls.
3) Take a ball and use your fingers to flatten it to the shape of a disk. Keep it thicker at the centre.

4) Put one or two tablespoon of stuffing in the centre.
5) Pinch the edges all around to form sharp bumps. The ball should now look like a tiny container with a star-like shape.

6) Bring the edges together and form one tip.
7) Repeat the process to make enough modaks for everyone.

Answers: 1) d, 2) e, 3) b, 4) a, 5) c

ONAM

Onam is the official festival of Kerala and occurs in the month of Chingam (late August or early September). It starts with the star of Atham and lasts for ten days. The star of Thiruvonam is the tenth day. The festival is full of feasting, boat races, song, dance and merriment.

The Origin of Onam

Onam, or Thiruonam, originated as a joyous annual celebration honouring the golden rule of King Mahabali, a mythical king who ruled Kerala a very long time ago. It recalls the sacrifice of the great king, his true devotion to God, his human pride and his ultimate redemption. Onam welcomes the spirit of a great king and assures him that his people are happy and wish him well.

Facts and fables blend as Kerala celebrates this royal return, year after year, with the festivities of Onam. Legend has it that the gods plotted against Mahabali to end his reign. To accomplish this, they sent Lord Vishnu to Earth in the form of a dwarf Brahmin or Vamana. But before being trampled down to the netherworld, Vishnu granted the king's sole wish: to visit his land and people once every year. There are several other mythological stories surrounding the history and origin of this South Indian festival.

Onam Customs

A flower carpet called *pookalam* is laid in front of every house to welcome Mahabali. Earthen mounds representing Mahabali and Vishnu are placed in courtyards plastered with animal dung. Traditional rituals are performed, followed by a lavish feast called *sadhya.* Onam tradition also means new clothes for the whole family, sumptuous home-cooked delicacies on plantain leaves followed by sweets.

Spectacular parades of elephants, fireworks and the famous Kathakali dance are traditionally associated with Onam. It's also the season of many cultural and sports events and carnivals. All this makes Onam-time a perfect period to visit this coastal state, touted as God's Own Country. Because of the festival's popularity, the Government of Kerala has declared this time every year as Tourism Week.

The Grand Boat Race

One of the main attractions of Onam is the *Vallamkali,* or boat races of Karuvatta, Payippad, Aranmula and Kottayam. Hundreds of oarsmen row traditional boats to the rhythm of drums and cymbals. These long and graceful snake boats, called *Chundan*s, are named after their long hulls and high sterns that resemble the raised hood of a cobra.

Other types of boats are also popular at this time. *Odis* are small and swift and adorned with gold tasseled silk umbrellas. *Churulan*s have elaborately curled prows and sterns. And the *Veppu*s is a kind of cook-boat.

Thousands throng the banks to cheer and watch the breathtaking show of rowing skills. These boats – all pitted against their own kind – rip through the backwaters of Kerala in a tussle of speed.

Onam is for One and All

Although this festival has its origin in Hindu mythology, Onam is for all people of all classes and creeds. Hindus, Muslims and Christians, the wealthy and the downtrodden, all celebrate Onam with equal fervor. The secular character of Onam is unique to Kerala.

Here is the traditional legend association with the Onam festival.

Homecoming of King Mahabali

According to legend, a long time ago, an Asura or demon king called Mahabali ruled Kerala. He was a wise, benevolent and judicious ruler, his subjects loved him. Soon his fame as an able king began to spread far and wide, but when he extended his rule to the heavens and the netherworld, the gods and demons began to fear his growing powers.

Presuming that he might become over-powerful, Aditi, the mother of Devas pleaded with Lord Vishnu to curtail Mahabali's powers. Vishnu transformed himself into a dwarf named Vamana and approached Mahabali while he was performing a *yajna* and asked Mahabali for alms. Being a generous king, Mahabali granted him a wish.

Mahabali's preceptor, Sukracharya warned him against making the gift. He had realized that the seeker was no ordinary person. But Mahabali's ego was boosted to think that God had asked him for a favour. So, he firmly declared that there is no greater sin than going back on one's promise. Mahabali kept his word and granted Vamana his wish.

The Vamana asked for a simple gift – three paces of land and the king agreed to it. Vamana – who was Vishnu in the guise of one of his ten avatars – then increased his stature. With the first step covered the sky, blotting out the stars. With this the second step, straddled the netherworld. Realizing that Vamana's third step would destroy the Earth, Mahabali offered his head as a sacrifice to save the world.

Vishnu's third step pushed Mahabali to the netherworld. But before banishing him to the underworld, Vishnu granted him a boon. Since he was devoted to his kingdom and his people, Mahabali was allowed to return once a year from exile. That is the day of Thiruvonam.

ACTIVITIES

1 ALL HEADS AND NO TAILS

Craft an elephant head and use your favourite colours to make it your own.

You Need:

• Flat-bottomed thermocol plates • A pair of scissors • Glue • Paints • Paintbrushes

Make It!

1) Take two thermocol plates and cut off their rims, separating the flat surfaces from the textured boundaries.
2) On the flat surface cut-out of one plate, draw a pair of oval eyes with big black pupils and small eyebrows.
3) Use the boundaries of the two plates to make two ears and a trunk.
4) Glue them in their place – the ears on the sides and the trunk in place of a mouth.

5) Colour your elephant head however you want. It doesn't have to be grey. You may even add a little bow and make its cheeks pink.
6) Have fun with the activity!

2 SPRING RANGOLI

Use nature's colours to beautify your floor this Onam.

You Need:

- Flowers of different colours (marigolds, roses, chrysanthemums)

Make It!

1) You may use white chalk to draw concentric circles (circles within circles) on the floor. Or you can directly put the flowers in place.
2) Let orange or yellow flowers make up the central circle.
3) Use white flowers to make a circle around the central circle, and then red flowers around the white circle.
4) Use as many colours as you can acquire.
5) Feel free to change the order of colours!

3 TUB BOATING

You don't always need a boat to boat.

You Need:

- A small light plastic tub/basket • Rubber band
- Straw • Balloon • Bathtub or a large tub of water

Make It!

1) Pierce a small hole on one side of your small plastic tub. You can also use a plastic basket that has holes on its walls.

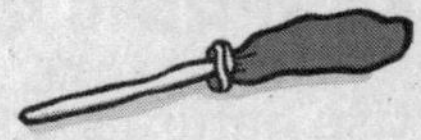

2) Put a straw inside a balloon and fasten it using a rubber band.

3) Place the balloon in your small tub/basket in such a way that the straw comes out from the hole you made previously.
4) Blow through the straw to fill the balloon up.

5) Immediately block the straw's open end with your thumb to stop the air from escaping.
6) Place your makeshift boat on one end of a big tub full of water.
7) Release your thumb and watch the boat go.

4 ONAM SNACK

Prepare easy and delicious banana chips to crunch on during the celebrations.

You Need:

• Two raw bananas • Salt
• Turmeric powder • Coconut Oil

Make It!

1) Ask an adult to slice the bananas into medium-thick chips.
2) Add one teaspoon of salt and two pinches of turmeric powder to some water. Mix it well.
3) Let the chips sit in turmeric water for a while and stir occasionally.
4) Drain the water completely.
5) Now, an adult can deep-fry the chips in coconut oil.
6) Serve the chips to your family.

5 FILL IN THE BLANKS

The words below are incomplete. Fill in the blank spaces to unravel the importance of Onam.

1) A legend behind Onam includes this deity and daitya — V___MA___A AND MA___A___AL___
2) Onam falls in this month of the Malayalam calendar — C___IN___A___
3) The floral rangoli made during Onam is called — P___OK___ ___LA___
4) This dance form is common during Onam — ___ULI___AL___

Answers:
1) Vamana and Mahabali, 2) Chingam, 3) Pookkalam, 4) Pulikali

DURGA PUJA

The conflict between the gods, or devas, and the demons, or *asuras*, have existed from time immemorial. Many asuras tried to overpower the gods and take over heaven. One such demon, Mahishasura, was half-buffalo and half-demon. He attained immense power as a result of a boon given by Agni, the fire God. Agni had told him that he could not be killed by a man. Only a woman could take his life. Mahishasura routinely troubled and tortured the gods in heaven.

When the gods pleaded to the trinity of Brahma, Vishnu and Shiva to take action against the tyranny of Mahishasura, the three decided to create a goddess who would possess the combined power of all the gods. Thus, Goddess Durga was born. She had ten arms, and all the gods gave their special weapons for each hand.

In a fierce and long battle that ensued, Durga, riding a lion, fought Mahishasura. The battle raged for nine days and nights. Finally on the tenth day of Ashvin Shukla Paksha, Mahishasura was defeated and slaughtered. Hence, the symbolic beheaded buffalo is seen below the idol of Goddess Durga.

Celebrating Durga Puja

In the east, Durga Puja is celebrated in a grand style. In Bengal, this is the biggest festival of the year. It is celebrated over five days as a community affair called Sarbojanin Puja. People dress up in new clothes. Beautiful pandals housing idols of Durga, accompanied by her children Lakshmi, Saraswati, Ganesha and Kartikeya, are constructed all over Bengal. In West Bengal, these pandals and the idols are usually designed around specific themes. These community pujas have large lunches and cultural programmes. On the tenth day, the idols are taken out in a procession and immersed in nearby lakes and rivers. After the immersion, it is time for Bijoya or Vijayadashami, when people visit each other's homes and exchange sweets and gifts.

In Orissa, women offer *dahi-pakhal* (cooked rice soaked in water, with curd), *pitha* (baked cakes), sweets and fried fish to Goddess Durga. And after the Bisarjan Jatra on the tenth day, and the immersion, people celebrate Ravana Podi during which they burn an effigy of Ravana.

The Birth of the Goddess

Goddess Durga was created to combat the evil demon Mahishasura. The trinity of Brahma, Vishnu and Shiva came together to create a powerful female form with ten arms.

Her face was created by Lord Shiva and her torso crafted by Indra. Her chest was made by Chandra and her teeth by Brahma. The lower part of her body was made by Bhudevi. Varuna sculpted her thighs and knees, and Agni created the Goddess's eyes. Thus, she was a supreme power created with a combination of the powers of all the other gods.

Then the gods gifted her their individual blessings and weapons. Armed like a warrior, the goddess rode into battle on a lion. After a fierce combat, Durga finally slew the demon king with her trident. Heaven and Earth rejoiced at her victory and peace was once again restored to the three worlds. The word 'Durga' in Sanskrit means a fort, or a secure and protected place. Another name for Durga is Durgatinashini which means 'the one who eliminates suffering'. Her name thus indicates her role as the one who protects her devotees and removes evil from the world.

There are numerous incarnations of Durga, including Kali, Bhagvati, Bhavani, Ambika, Lalita, Gauri, Kandalini, Java, Meenakshi and Kamakshi.

The Many Arms and Many Weapons of Durga

Durga is depicted as having ten arms. These represent the ten directions in Hinduism; she protects her devotees in all directions. In one hand she holds the conch-shell gifted to her by Varuna, God of the Sea. In two other hands she holds the bow and the arrow given to her by Vayu, the Wind God. One hand holds the thunderbolt of Indra, which can destroy anything it strikes without being affected. In yet another hand she holds the lotus, a symbol of spirituality and steadfastness. In another hand she holds the *sudarshan chakra*, which can destroy evil forces no matter how powerful they are. In her other hands she carries a longsword, and Brahma's *kamandalu* or a pot to carry holy water in. In her forearms she carries Shiva's all-powerful trident which is the weapon that provides the final death blow to Mahishasura.

The Nine Forms of the Goddess

The Goddess has nine forms known as Navadurga, all of which are worshipped during the nine days of the Navratri. Each represents different nuances and moods of the Mother Goddess.

Shailaputri: First Day

Shailaputri literally means the *putri*, or daughter, of the *shaila*, or mountains. Variously known as Sati, Bhavani, Parvati or Hemavati, this deity is the daughter of Hemavana – the king of the Himalayas. She rides a bull and carries a trident and a lotus in her two hands.

Bharmacharini: Second Day

Bharmacharini means one who practises great austerity. She holds a rosary in her right hand and a water utensil in her left. She is believed to endow happiness, peace, prosperity and grace upon all those who worship her.

Chandraghanta: Third Day

The Chandraghanta represents peace, tranquillity and prosperity. She has a *chandra* or half-moon on her forehead in the shape of a *ghanta*, or bell. That is why she is called Chandraghanta. She is the symbol of bravery and possesses great strength to fight all kinds of evil.

Kushmanda: Fourth Day

This avatar is considered the creator of the universe back when it was no more than a void full of darkness. Then the Goddess's light spread in all directions like rays from the sun. Kushmanda is depicted as having eight or ten hands.

Skanda Mata: Fifth Day

Skanda Mata, or the mother of Skanda or Lord Kartikeya, was chosen by gods as their commander-in-chief in the war against the demons. Skanda Mata has four arms and three eyes. She holds the infant Skanda in her right upper arm and a lotus in her right hand. The left upper arm is poised to grant boons and the left lower hand holds a lotus.

Katyayani: Sixth Day

Kata was a sage who underwent long austerities and penance in order to receive the grace of the Mother Goddess. As a result of his devotion, he was blessed with a daughter who was a goddess. Thus, the Goddess Katyayani was born to Kata as an avatar of Durga herself.

Kaal Ratri: Seventh Day

This mighty and frightening aspect of Durga has a dark complexion, wild hair and a fearless posture. A necklace of lightning adorns her neck. She has three eyes that shine bright and terrible flames emanate from her breath. Her vehicle is the donkey. She is black like Maha Kali and holds a sparkling sword in her right hand. She is supposed to represent freedom from fear and troubles.

Maha Gauri: Eighth Day

She is intelligent, peaceful and calm. Due to her long austerities in Himalayan forests, she developed a dark complexion. After Lord Shiva cleaned her with the water of the Ganges, her body regained its beauty. She then came to be known as Maha Gauri, which means extremely white. She wears white clothes, has four arms and rides on a bull.

Siddhidatri: Ninth Day

Siddhidatri is the ninth form of the goddess. She is worshipped on the ninth day of Navaratri and has great healing powers. She has four arms and carries a chakra, a mace, a conch-shell and a lotus in them.

ACTIVITIES

1 BALLOON FLOWER BASKET

Make a lovely little basket to keep puja flowers in.

You Need:

• A round balloon • Short lengths of thick yarn (like wool or string) and ribbon • Glue • Heavy paper • Stapler • A pair of scissors • A shallow bowl

Make It!

1) Blow up a balloon.
2) Pour some glue into a shallow bowl. Dip pieces of yarn and ribbon in glue and wrap them around the blown-up balloon. Wrap in all different direction to form a kind of web. Let the glue dry overnight.
3) After the glue has dried, pop the balloon and peel it away from the yarn and ribbon pieces.
4) Cut off the top to make the mouth of your basket.
5) Make a base: Cut a strip of heavy paper. Staple it to make a ring. Glue a strip of ribbon around it.

Squeeze glue along the top edge and set your basket on it.

6) Make a top: Glue a similar strip of paper-and-ribbon at the top to make your basket sturdy.

2 PANCHAMRUTAM

Literally an offering to the gods! This prasad or naivedyam has five magical ingredients. It is said to be great favourites of the gods.

You Need:

• ½ cup dahi • ¼ cup milk • 2 tbsp honey
• 2 mashed bananas • ½ teaspoon ghee

Make It!

Mix all the ingredients together. Yum . . . now you know why the gods are so pleased!

3 YOUR OWN GODS

You can make just anything with this wonderful dough. Make the dough and then fashion into the shape of any idols you want!

You Need:

• Mixing bowl • 1¼ cup flour • ¾ cup water
• 1 tbsp vegetable oil • 1¼ cup salt
• Clear varnish
• Paintbrush

Make It!

1) Pour the flour, water, vegetable oil and salt in the mixing bowl. Blend well together using your hands. Form the mixture into a soft dough ball. Add a little water from time to time to make it wet.
2) Sprinkle some flour on the dough. Continue to knead until the dough is smooth and stretchable. Your modelling clay is ready.
3) Now model it into any god's shape. When it's completely dry and hard, you can paint it as you like.
4) With a thick paintbrush, add a coat of varnish to protect your handiwork.

4 FLOWER CENTREPIECE

You can keep this pretty centerpiece on the festive dinner table and earn compliments!

You Need:

• Dried pressed flowers • Green chart paper
• A pair of scissors • Glue

Make It!

1) Press flowers between newspapers kept under a heavy book.
2) Cut a rectangular piece of chart paper. Draw five or six lines at equal distances. Cut along the lines.
3) Decorate the strips with the dried flowers by sticking them down carefully.
4) Now join the two ends of the chart paper together using glue or staples, and bend the 'stems' down.
5) If you don't want to use dried flowers, you can make flower shapes with small coloured buttons or even paper.

5 DECO PLATES

Use these decorative plates for puja knick-knacks.

You Need:

• Terracotta plates • Ideas!

Make It!

Ideas for decorating terracotta plates:

1) Paint them with little dabs using leftover nail-polish – the more glittery the better.

2) Stick mirrors into designs painted with acrylic colours or poster colours (if what you keep in them is going to be dry stuff).
3) Dip leaves in paint (kept in a shallow dish) and print on the plates for a beautiful 'natural' pattern.
4) Cut designs in a round piece of paper and line the plate with it.
5) Stick shiny golden and silver braids in a radiating design from the centre.

6 MARBLE ROLLING WRAPPING PAPER

Make beautiful wrapping paper without losing your marbles!

You Need:

• Plain paper • Spoon • Small bowls • Marbles • Poster paints • A lid of a cardboard box

Make It!

1) Pour paint into dishes and drop two or three marbles into each colour.
2) Tape down your 'wrapping' paper (at the corners) inside the box lid.
3) Lift out the marbles with a spoon and set them on the paper taped in the box lid.
4) Tip the box lid this way and that so that the marbles roll around. When the paint is used, dunk the marbles back into the paint and add new colours.

NAVRATRI AND DUSSEHRA

The festival of Dussehra is celebrated in September or October on the tenth day of the Hindu autumn lunar month of Ashvin. The Navaratri or Nine Nights start after the Shukla Paksha Pratipada, or the day after the new moon. It continues till Dashami, the tenth day of Ashvin. Dussehra is the conclusion of these festive days. The festival is celebrated as the victory of good over evil. It's also known as Vijayadashami, Dasara and Dashahara.

According to the Ramayana, on this day Rama, the prince of Ayodhya, killed the demon king Ravana. Ravana had forcibly carried away Rama's wife Sita to his kingdom of Lanka. Rama, his brother Lakshmana, their follower Hanuman and his army of *vanaras* (monkeys) had then fought a great battle to rescue Sita.

Rama had performed Chandi Homa, a ceremony to invoke Goddess Durga. The goddess had blessed Rama and also shared knowledge on how to defeat and kill Ravana. On the day of Ashvin Shukla Dashami, Rama and his army defeated Ravana. That is why, on Dussehra, effigies of Ravana, his brother Kumbhakarna and son Meghanad are burnt at sunset.

Many people perform *homas* and recite the Sundara Kanda section of the Ramayana for nine days. These rituals are meant to rid the home of the ten bad qualities represented by ten heads of Ravana. They are *kama* (lust), *krodha* (anger), *moha* (delusion), *lobha* (greed), *mada* (pride), *maatsyasya* (envy), *manas* (mind), *buddhi* (intellect), *chitta* (will) and *ahamkara* (ego).

Celebrating Dussehra in North India

This festival of fun is unique because it is celebrated at the same time in different parts of the country in different ways. Durga Puja and Dussehra are also celebrated by Indians living in different parts of the world and these festivals have adapted to all kinds of cultures.

For nine days before Dussehra, people celebrate the festival of Navaratri. It is a time for strict fasting. Devotees have a special kind of *navratra* diet. In Kashmir, Himachal Pradesh, western Uttar Pradesh and Uttarakhand, people plant barley seeds in earthen pots on the first day of Navaratri. On the day of Dussehra, the nine-day old sprouts (called *noratra*s or *norta*s) are used as lucky items. Men place them in their caps or behind their ears!

Huge celebrations happen on Dussehra, with the Ramlila as a centrepiece. Large effigies of Ravana are set aflame with firecrackers. Fairs take place and are full of fun games and food stalls. Street plays and puppet shows are performed. They celebrate Rama's victory over the evil king. In cities like Varanasi, Dussehra overlaps with Ramlila or the Rama Drama. During this time, the city is full of performances of traditional plays with scenes from the Ramayana.

Celebrating Navratri and Dandiya Raas in Western India

In western India, the nine days of Navratri are given a fun twist. People spend evenings dancing and singing. A special kind of choreographed dance with coloured sticks, called Dandiya Raas, is performed. Both men and women dress in colourful outfits and participate in pairs for the Dandiya Raas. The *dandiya*s or sticks are made of bamboo and have little bells at the ends. They make a tinkling sound when they hit another. The sticks are believed to represent the swords of Goddess Durga and thus they have special significance during this time. The dancers begin with a slow tempo, and then move faster and faster. That way, each person in a circle performs a solo dance with his/her own sticks and also strikes his partner's *dandiya*s in style!

Apart from Dandiya, the women also perform the Garba, a group dance with much clapping and synchronized twirls. Women usually dress up in beautifully embroidered *choli-ghagra* with *bandhani* prints and dance in circles around a pot containing a lamp.

Celebrating Navratri and Dussehra in South India

In the south, the nine days before Dasara, as they call it there, are dedicated to the worship of Durga, Lakshmi and Saraswati. During Navratri, many households display and pray dolls and other figurines called Golu or Bommai Kalu. They represent figures from mythology. People light lamps in front of them and draw rangolis with dry colours and rice powder. Special goodies are offered to the Golus and they are worshipped till Vijayadashami. The tenth day is regarded as an auspicious day to begin a child's education as it is dedicated to the goddess of learning, Saraswati. The Dussehra celebrations in Mysore are a treat to watch.

Chamundi, a form of Durga, has been the family deity of the Maharaja of Mysore and is worshipped in royal style. Chamundeshwari is taken around Mysore in a procession on a golden *ambari* or elephant-mounted throne, with horses and courtiers to her hilltop temple.

In Karnataka and Andhra Pradesh, the Ayudh Puja is observed on the ninth day. Vijayadashami Day is believed to be lucky for starting all new ventures or buying something new. On the river banks of the Krishna river at Vijayawada, thousands of people visit the Sri Durga Malleswar Swami temple. The celebrations conclude on the tenth day with the Teppa Utsavam, in which Durga's image is placed on a big boat decorated with flowers and lights.

ACTIVITIES

1 MAKE A *RANGOLI*

Rangoli making is a very old art, mentioned in ancient texts. These designs were said to please the gods. There are different types of rangolis: *alpana* in Bengal and *kolam* in Tamil Nadu are made with wet paste. *Muggu* in Andhra Pradesh is made with dry powder.

You Need:

• Rice • Water • Muslin cloth

Traditional rangoli paste

White: Soak one small bowl of rice in water overnight. Dry and grind it to a fine powder. If you want to make a wet rangoli, add just enough water to make it of a pouring consistency.

Yellow: Add ground turmeric to the paste.

Orange: Add *gulal* from your leftover Holi colours, or add *sindoor*.

Red: Add *kumkum*.

For wet patterns dip a piece of fine muslin cloth into the paste. Hold it in your palm and let the paste drip from your index finger along the outlines of the pattern on the floor.

Working with powder is difficult at first, but it's fun when you get the hang of it.

1) For lines, pick the powder between your thumb and forefinger and run your thumb up the forefinger while you go along a line.
2) To fill in, drop some powder into the area and use your fingertips to pat it in place.

It's easy to draw a rangoli pattern using a grid. Try it!

2 QUICK COCONUT BALLS

Mmm . . . easy and tasty . . . this recipe will get you the title of Junior Masterchef!

You Need:

- 2/3 can of condensed milk
- 250 gms desiccated coconut

Make It!

1) Put the condensed milk in the fridge for a few hours. This makes the mixing easier.
2) Put aside two to three tablespoons of the desiccated coconut.
3) Take out the condensed milk and put it in a pan. Mix the remaining desiccated coconut in it.

4) Once the coconut is well mixed, wash and then grease your palms with a little oil or butter. Roll the mix into little balls.
5) Roll each of the coconut balls in the desiccated coconut you kept aside earlier.
6) Keep the coconut balls in the fridge for an hour before serving.

3 MAKE RAVANA AT HOME WITH SCRAPS

Yes, you can make your own and burn him up, too. Please make sure that grown-ups are present when you set fire to your Ravana.

You Need:

- Shoeboxes
- Bits and pieces of paper junk
- Ten paper plates
- Paints or bits of coloured paper
- Leftover sparklers from last year

Make It!

1) Pile up three or four shoeboxes any which way you want. The open side should face away from you.
2) Staple ten paper plates together and draw Ravana faces on each one.
3) Now stick the fifth paper plate on the top shoebox.
4) Fill the boxes with all sorts of throwaway paper junk. Add the sparklers too.
5) Call the grown-ups to light your Ravana – and watch him burn!

4 RAVANA MASK

Make this simple Ravana mask for yourself or your kid brother/sister.

You Need:

• Ten paper plates, preferably one large one and nine smaller ones • Crayons or paints • Odds and end to decorate with • A pair of scissors • Stapler • Short length of string

Make It!

1) Draw and colour a scary Ravana face on the large paper plate.
2) Make two holes on either side and tie a small length of string on each side to tie the mask on your face.
3) Copy the face on to all the other paper plates. You could get each of your friends to draw and colour the other nine faces. That will make your Ravana mask more interesting!

4) Now staple five smaller plates one after the other to one side of the large Ravana face, and four on the other side.
5) Wear the mask and amuse everyone with your Ravana laughter . . . HAHAHA!

5 FESTIVAL QUOTIENT

Test your festival quotient with these questions.

1) Who was the original writer of the Ramayana?
2) Which is the state where Durga is said to have killed Mahishasura, an incident from which the state also got its name?
3) Which famous national song of our country was inspired by Goddess Durga?
4) Which is the famous book on which most Ramlila scripts are based?
5) What do you call the auspicious string of mango leaves people put up on doorways during Navaratri?

6 CRUMPLE WRAP

A cool wrapping paper idea!

You Need:

• Newspaper • Paints • Shallow Dishes for paint
• Thick sheet of paper

Make It!

1) Crumple a sheet of newspaper into a ball and dip it into a shallow dish of paint.

2) Pat the newspaper all over a piece of thick paper. The wrinkled paper creates a lovely crackle pattern.
3) When your newspaper gets too soggy, throw it away and crumple up a fresh piece.

7 STATE IT QUIZ

Answer these questions and see how high your festival geography is!

Name the state or place where Dussehra/Navratri is celebrated as (unscramble the letters to get the right answer):

1) 'Homecoming of the Daughter' (STEW BANGLE)

____

2) The time when images of many gods are brought together in decorated palanquins and a grand fair is held (LIMCAHAH SHARPED)

____

3) A period of strict fasting (BANJUP)

____

4) the time when one greets friends and relatives by exchanging *sami* or *bengaru* leaves (YAHMAD REPDASH, RYSOME and NARADH SHEPARD)

____

Answers: 1) West Bengal, 2) Himachal Pradesh, 3) Punjab, 4) Madhya Pradesh, Mysore and Andhra Pradesh

Answers: 1) Valmiki, 2) Mysuru, 3) 'Vande Mataram' by Bankim Chandra Chatterjee, 4) Tulsidas's Ramacharitmanas, 5) Toran

DIWALI

Each legend of Diwali describes the victory of good over evil.

The essence of Diwali is captured in the famous verse from the *Brihadaranyaka Upanishad*, 'Asato ma sad gamaya, Tamaso ma jyotir gamaya, Mrityor ma amritam gamaya,' which means 'Lead us from the unreal to the real, lead us from darkness to light, lead us from death to immortality.'

In this sense, Diwali leads us from darkness to light – a light that empowers us to do good deeds. During Diwali, lights illuminate every corner of India and the scent of incense sticks hangs in the air, mingled with the cheer of joy, togetherness and hope.

The Origin of Diwali: Myths and Legends

The origin of Diwali can be traced back to ancient India, when it was probably an important harvest festival. However, there are several myths and legends about the origin of Diwali.

Diwali commemorates the return of Lord Rama along with Sita and Lakshmana from their fourteen-year exile after defeating the demon-king Ravana. In joyous celebration of the return of their king, the people of Ayodhya, the capital of Lord Rama's kingdom, illuminated it with earthen diyas or oil lamps.

Some believe it to be the celebration of the wedding of Lakshmi with Lord Vishnu. Lakshmi, the goddess of wealth, was reborn on the new moon day of the Hindu Kartik month (October–November in the western calendar) during the fabled churning of the ocean or *Samudra-Manthan* on Diwali.

Lord Ganesha, the elephant-headed God, a symbol of auspiciousness and wisdom, is also worshiped in most Hindu homes on this day. In Bengal, the festival is dedicated to the worship of Mother Kali, the dark goddess of strength.

Diwali in Indian History

One of the greatest of Hindu Kings, Vikramaditya, was crowned on Diwali day, making it a day of historical importance. It marked the beginning of the Vikram Era or Vikram Samvat in the Hindu calendar system.

According to the Mahabharata, the Pandavas were banished for twelve years after they were defeated by the Kauravas at a game of dice. It is believed that they returned from their exile on Diwali and their subjects celebrated the day by lighting earthen lamps. Among Jains, Diwali has an added significance as the Lord Mahavira attained the eternal bliss of nirvana on this day.

The third Sikh Guru, Amar Das, made Diwali a Red-Letter Day when all Sikhs would gather to receive the Guru's blessings. The foundation stone of the Golden Temple at Amritsar was laid on Diwali day in 1577. On the occasion of Diwali in 1619, the sixth Sikh Guru, Hargobind, who was held by the Mughal Emperor Jahangir, was released from the Gwalior Fort along with fifty-two imprisoned kings.

In 1999, Pope John Paul II performed a special mass in an Indian church where the altar was decorated with Diwali lamps. The Pope had a tilak marked on his forehead and his sermon was peppered with references to the festival of light.

The Four Days of Diwali

Each day of Diwali has a legend associated with it.

The first day of the festival, Naraka Chaturdasi, marks the defeat of the demon king Narakarsura by Lord Krishna and his wife Satyabhama. On the day preceding Diwali, Krishna killed Narakasura and rescued 16,000 women from his captivity. The celebration of this freedom went on for two days, including Diwali day, as a victory festival. In south India, people take an oil bath in the morning, wear new clothes, distribute sweets and light diyas in the evening to mark the destruction of Narakasura.

Amavasya, the second day of Diwali, marks the worship of Lakshmi in her most benevolent mood, fulfilling the wishes of her devotees. Amavasya is also related to the story of Lord Vishnu, who in his dwarf incarnation (Vamanavatara) defeated the tyrant Bali and banished him to hell. Bali was allowed to return to Earth once a year, to light millions of lamps to drive out darkness and ignorance and spread the radiance of love and wisdom.

It is on the third day of Diwali, Kartika Shudda Padyami, that the Asura king Bali steps out of the underworld and rules the Earth according to the boon given to him by Lord Vishnu.

The fourth day is referred to as Yama Dvitiya or Bhai Dooj and on this day, sisters invite their brothers to their homes and tie sacred threads on their wrists, denoting their love for their siblings.

The day after Diwali is celebrated in many parts of India as the beginning of a new year in the Vikram Era. Known as Annakut (*anna* meaning grain or food and *kut* meaning mountain or large pile), it signals a new beginning with a golden harvest of the crop that had been planted during and after the monsoon season. The new crop is cut and offered to the gods on the first day of this new year.

SIGNIFICANCE OF DIWALI TRADITIONS

Lights and Firecrackers

All the simple rituals of Diwali have a greater significance.

The illumination of homes with lights and the skies with firecrackers was originally meant to show respect to the gods for giving us wealth and prosperity. According to one belief, the sound of firecrackers is an indication of the joy of the people living on Earth, making the gods aware of their plentiful state.

There is another reason behind the lights and firecrackers. This one has a more scientific basis: the fumes produced by the crackers kill a lot of insects and mosquitoes, found in plenty after the rains. However, this old idea seems to have backfired in recent times as the increase in the number of firecrackers has added to the perils of air and noise pollution. In 2018, the courts in India placed a ban on the sale and production of all crackers except 'green crackers' and also those which have reduced emissions.

Dhanteras or *Chhoti* Diwali

The festival of Dhanteras (*dhan* meaning wealth and *teras* meaning thirteenth) is celebrated two days before the festival of lights.

An ancient legend ascribes the celebration of Dhanteras to an interesting story about the sixteen-year-old son of King Hima. His horoscope predicted his death by snakebite on the fourth day of his marriage. On that particular day, his newly wed wife did not allow him to sleep. She laid out all her ornaments and lots of gold and silver coins in a heap at the entrance of the sleeping chamber and lit lamps all over the place. Then she narrated stories and sang songs to keep her husband from falling asleep.

The next day, when Yama, the god of death, arrived at the prince's doorstep in the guise of a serpent, his eyes were dazzled by the brilliance of the lamps and jewellery. Yama could not enter the prince's chamber, so he climbed on top of the heap of gold coins and sat there the entire night listening to the stories and songs. In the morning, he silently went away.

Thus, the young prince was saved from death by the cleverness of his new bride, and the day came to be celebrated as Dhanteras. Since this is the night before Diwali, it is also called *Chhoti* Diwali or Small Diwali.

Colour me!

ACTIVITIES

1 DIYA MOBILE

This lovely Diwali decoration will put you in the festive spirit and you can hang it in your room for as long as you want just because it is so pretty!

You Need:

• Yellow textured or handmade paper • Red or any other bright textured or handmade paper • Gold thread • Gold glitter glue

Make It!

1) Cut out a flame from yellow paper and a diya shape from your other paper.
2) Make a hole at the bottom of the flame and another at the end of the diya.
3) Tie them together with the gold thread.
4) Make a hole at the top of the flame and tie on a gold cord to hang.

Make patterns on the flame with glitter glue. Hang to catch the light!

2 GLASS CANDLE HOLDER

This tea light candle holder can be used to decorate your house on Diwali or when you simply want your house or room to look all dressed up.

You Need:

• An old jam jar • Coloured wire • Glass paint

Make It!

1) Wrap the wire tightly around the top of the jar, then make a loop over the top of the jar to make a handle. You may also want to ask an adult to help you with this.
2) Pass the wire back over the rim to make another loop. Twist the two loops together.
3) Wrap the wire around again and twist the end on to some of the other coils of wire to secure everything in place.
4) Decorate the jar with glass paints. You can use Diwali themes to make your jar as colourful and decorative as you like. Match it with your house's colour scheme or just paint it your favourite shade.
5) Put a tea light into the jar and ask an adult to help you light it.

3 THE DRAWING PIN AND SEQUINNED CANDLE

This innovative candle will stand tall among others of its kind.

You Need:

• A big fat plain coloured candle • Multi-coloured drawing pins • Silver and golden drawing pins

Make It!

1) Push the pins into the candle in different designs.
2) Alternate the gold and silver with the multi-coloured ones until the design is complete.
3) Alternate the gold and silver with the multi-coloured ones until the design is complete.

4 CLAY DIYA

This pretty homemade diya can be used for the puja thali or for general decoration near your door and windows.

You Need:

• Air-drying clay • Baking or parchment paper
• Mixed flower petals • Tea light • An old tea cup
• Paints • Varnish

Make It!

1) Take some clay and shape it into a small bowl over the bottom of a cup. Press the petals into the outside of the bowl. Leave the clay to dry.
2) Use paints to paint around the flowers.
3) Varnish the whole diya and over the flowers as well.
4) Let it dry. Put a tea light inside the bowl and watch your diya light up your home.

5 DIWALI SWEET TREATS

While there will be plenty of *mithai* and halwa doing the rounds on Diwali, here is an easy and tasty chocolate treat that you can share with your friends and relatives and earn extra brownie points for taste and novelty.

You Need:

• 6 ripe bananas • 1 cup chocolate chips (or drinking chocolate powder) • Some clean wooden sticks/toothpicks

Make It!

1) Peel bananas; cut in half crosswise or in four parts criss-cross.
2) Insert a wooden stick or toothpick into the flat end of each banana half.
3) Put the bananas on a tray and leave it in the freezer for about three hours.
4) Melt chocolate chips in a bowl in the microwave.
5) With a spatula or large spoon, quickly spread the melted chocolate over each banana, coating each piece well.
6) Chocolate will become firm right away, coming in contact with cold bananas. Make thick coats.
7) Wrap each banana in foil and store in the freezer with the toothpicks still inside.
8) Serve chilled when the guests arrive and watch the treats disappear.

6 ROCKET BOOKMARK

This is a perfect bookmark to remind you of the festival after it is over and is also a good gift for friends.

You Need:

• Felt paper in two colours • Ice cream sticks • Glue • Tinsel • Star-shaped Sequins • A pair of scissors

Make It!

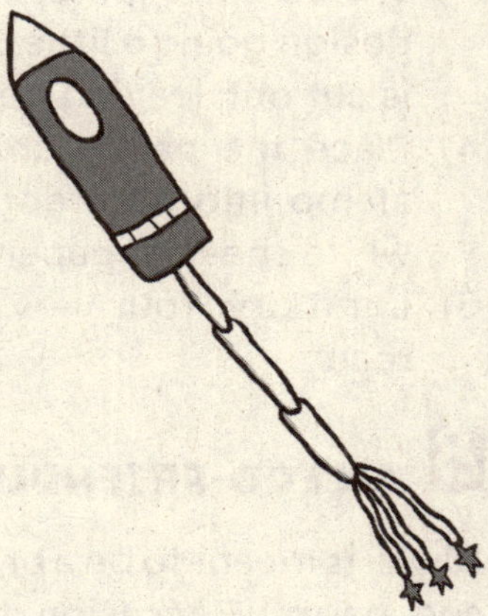

1) Cut out a triangle and a rectangle from the felt paper. Glue the triangle to the top of the rectangle. Glue the ice cream stick to the bottom of the rectangle.
2) Glue two more ice cream sticks to the bottom of the rocket.
3) Glue the tinsel and sequinned stars to the ice cream stick.
4) Dry it out before using it as a bookmark!

7 DIWALI WRAPPING PAPER

Diwali is an occasion to exchange gifts and this potato stamp wrapping paper is perfect to put everyone in a festive mood.

You Need:

• Paints • A potato • A blunt knife • Drawing paper • White crepe or handmade paper

Make It!

1) Cut the potato in half and trace its shape onto the paper.
2) Draw a diya or a rocket within that shape.
3) Cut the shape out and put on top of the potato half. With a blunt knife, score around the edge of your design going a little deeper so that the extra potato is cut out, leaving behind only your design.
4) Place the paints on a plate and dip your potato stamp into different paints and place all over the white sheet of paper.
5) Let it dry. Your very own Diwali wrapping paper is ready.

8 AN ECO-FRIENDLY DIWALI

Diwali is meant to be a bright festival and not a polluting and harmful occasion that destroys our planet, our health and harms animals. Here are four tips through which you can celebrate a bright, peaceful and eco-friendly Diwali and still have fun!

Go Natural

Instead of bursting crackers, light diyas all around your house and neighbourhood. It is much prettier and more fulfilling. You can plant trees on every Diwali morning instead of lighting fireworks.

Set a Time Limit

Even while celebrating with extended families and friends, remember to set a time limit of two to three hours for bursting firecrackers. This way you will reduce noise pollution and let the sick and elderly rest in the night.

Help Animals in Your Neighbourhood

Dogs, cats and birds have a terrible time during Diwali due to the loud noise and high levels of smoke in the atmosphere. Help them out by making some space in your garden or backyard for some of them. Keep some old newspapers and old rags in cardboard boxes so that they can burrow in and cover their ears. Keep an eye out for all those mischief makers who torment animals during this festival by tying crackers to their tail and sound them off. Or call your nearest animal welfare organization if you see such cruelty taking place.

Cut Down on Spending and Give

Instead of going overboard buying things for yourself and your house on Diwali, get together with your friends and pool a part of your spending money to buy some new clothes or toys for an orphanage, or simply donate the money to a charity after consulting your parents.

BHAI DOOJ

The bond between brothers and sisters has a special place in Indian culture. People celebrate this relationship twice every year with the festivals of Rakshabandhan and Bhai Dooj.

What, When and How

After the high voltage celebrations of Diwali, the festival of lights and firecrackers, brothers and sisters all over India get ready for Bhai Dooj. Sisters demonstrate their love by putting an auspicious tilak or tika – a dot made of vermilion or sandalwood paste – on the forehead of their brothers and perform the ritual of aarti for them. Gifts are exchanged as well.

Bhai Dooj is celebrated on the fifth and last day of Diwali. The name 'Dooj' means the second day after the new moon, the day of the festival, and 'bhai' means 'brother'.

Myths and Legends

Bhai Dooj is also called Yama Dwiteeya as it's believed that on this day, Yamaraj, the Lord of Death, visits his sister Yamuna. She puts the auspicious tilak on his forehead and prays for his well-being. So, it's believed that anyone who receives a tilak from his sister on this day will never be thrown into hell.

According to another legend, on this day, Lord Krishna, after slaying the Narakasura demon, went to meet his sister Subhadra. She welcomed him with lamps, flowers and sweets. She also greeted with by applying the *tika* on her brother's forehead before letting him into her house.

Yet another story is that of Lord Mahavira, the founder of Jainism. When he attained nirvana, his brother, King Nandivardhan, was distressed because he missed him. He was comforted by their sister, Sudarshana. Bhai Dooj, according to this story, is a celebration of this sibling love.

Special Celebration in Bengal

In Bengal, Bhai Dooj is called 'Bhai Phonta'. The sister fasts until she applies a *phonta* or mark with sandalwood paste on her brother's forehead, offers him sweets and gifts and prays for his long and healthy life.

Every brother eagerly awaits this occasion as it is an opportunity for a good feast. Gifts are also enthusiastically exchanged and merriment follows with the sound of conch shells in every Bengali household.

What's Important about Bhai Dooj

Like all other Indian festivals, Bhai Dooj too has a lot to do with family ties and social attachments. It serves as a good time, especially for children, and for the whole family to continue sharing the joy after Diwali.

Sometimes, sisters who are unable to meet their brothers in person, send their *tika* in an envelope by post. Virtual tilaks and Bhai Dooj e-cards have made it even easier for brothers and sisters who live far away from each other to greet their siblings on this occasion.

ACTIVITIES

1 THE STORY OF YOUR LIVES

All you need to really make your sibling's Bhai Dooj perfect!

You Need:

• Colourful paper • Pencils • Needle and thread
• Ruler • Colour pencils, crayons • A pair of scissors
• Lots of old memories

Make It!

1) The first thing you need to do is write the story of your lives together. Write about the best memories you have with your siblings, your favourite hobbies, all your favourite foods, your favourite holidays, movies you love watching together, all of it!
2) According to the amount you have written, figure out the size of your book.
3) You will be folding the paper in half and sewing it up the middle, so the paper needs to be twice as long as you want each page to be.

4) Take a ruler and measure a line separating your pages exactly in half. Then place a dot at one-inch intervals so your stitching will be even.
5) Thread enough string so you have three times the line's length. Start at the bottom, leaving four inches of thread for tying a knot when you are finished. Now push the needle through the paper.
6) Go up the book following the line, with big stitches at every dot.
7) Once you reach the top, go back down by following the line again. Repeat this one more time.
8) And presto! You have made a bound book which your sibling will treasure for the rest of their lives!

2 SPANISH GIANT PAPER MASK

These masks sit on top of your sibling's head and are often used in Spanish carnivals. Now give your own version of this as a beautiful Bhai Dooj gift.

You Need:

• A balloon • Liquid glue • Water • Vaseline • Newspaper • An old tennis ball • Paints • Coloured strips of paper

Make It!

1) Inflate a balloon and tie a knot at the end. Put some petroleum jelly or Vaseline all over the balloon.

2) Make some papier-mâché glue by adding equal measures of glue and water.
3) Cover the balloon with the glue you have made and paste some newspaper on it. Do three layers of this.

4) Leave it aside to dry.
5) Once dry and hard, deflate the balloon (by pricking it with a pin). Pull it out of the shell.
6) Cut an old tennis ball in half and glue each half on to the shell you have made to make the eyes of the mask.

7) Paint the mask.
8) Paint the half tennis balls to make the eyes. Make a mouth as well with paint.
9) Trim the base of the mask so that it sits on the top of your head. Make little holes on either side of the base of the mask. Attach a piece of elastic in the holes and around your chin and tie the mask in place over your head. Or you can stick it onto a hairband.

3 PHOTO PROJECT

People all over the world are photographing one particular thing every day for days, months and even years. This can become the best gift for your sibling on Bhai Dooj.

You Need:

• Camera • Computer with Adobe Photoshop
• Your sibling's beautiful face!

Make It!

1) Take a picture of your sibling every morning, as soon as they wake up, or just before they do. It will be nice if you can get the same pose. But if not, just take a 'mug-shot', a shot of their face. Notice any changes in their face with the passing time?
2) Use a software like Adobe Photoshop and stitch all your photographs together into the coolest photocollage ever! All you need to do is place the pictures chronologically next to each other.
3) Print out on photographic paper. And if you have time enough before the big day, ask your parents to frame it.

4 STOP MOTION ANIMATION

Does you sibling bore you on normal days? On Bhai Dooj, animate them!

You Need:

• A camera • A computer with PowerPoint
• Your sibling!

Make It!

1) Stop-Motion animation is much simpler than it sounds, but it can be tedious. An object is moved very slightly between camera frames, giving the illusion of motion.
2) Try it first with a doll. Take a photograph of the doll standing straight.
3) Now move the hand very slightly and take another photograph. Turn the hand completely around, taking as many photographs in short intervals along the way.
4) Be careful to take the photographs from the same angle throughout.
5) Put all the photos into a slideshow with less than five seconds per slide. You will have your first stop-motion animation film!
6) Now, get your sibling to pose. Get him or her to wave at the camera, but to do it very slowly. First get them to raise their arms, then get them to change it very slowly, and take as many snaps at every position, as you can.
7) Put them all together in a slideshow, and you have your very own stop motion film!

5 WHO AM I?

The perfect game for when all your cousins and family come home for Bhai Dooj.

You Need:

• Post-its • Names of famous people

Play It!

1) Give all the players sheets of Post-its with names of famous people on them.
2) Each player pastes the Post-it on his/her forehead. Thus, each player knows the identity of every other player, except their own.
3) Each player then asks the group 'yes' or 'no' questions (like twenty questions). The object of the game is to guess which famous person you are.
4) Take turns and go around the circle.
5) For the next round, keep your pad of Post-its ready. Have each person write down one famous person's name and hand it to the person sitting to the right of him or her.
6) Keep going till your cousins need to leave!

6 LIMERICK YOUR GIFT

Get away by giving your siblings something nice and cheap!

You Need:

• Pen • Paper • Your imagination!

Do It!

1) There was a poet called Edward Lear who made limericks very popular, though people had been

writing them much earlier. They have five lines. The first two lines rhyme with each other and with the fifth line. And the third and the fourth lines rhyme with each other.

2) The first line usually begins 'There was a young (or old) man or woman (or boy or girl) of somewhere'. Then you think of a rhyme for the second line. That gives you an idea for the last line. There are two short lines in between.

For instance:

My sister will
push and shove,
She was no angel sent from above,
A pinch here and a kick there,
Then a pull on my short black hair,
Yet somehow I still manage to love.

Complete these limericks by filling in the blanks with your own ideas and words.

There was an alien from Outer Space who said, 'I

want to go to a place where there are ____________

And ____________

This planet is such a disgrace!

Now all you need to do is write one with your brother or sister in it!

CHHATH

Chhath also called Dala Puja is a Hindu festival popular in the Northern and Eastern Indian states of Bihar and Jharkhand and even Nepal. The word 'Chhath' has its origin in 'sixth' as it is celebrated on the sixth day or 'Shasthi' of the lunar fortnight of Kartik (October–November) in the Hindu calendar – six days after Diwali, the festival of lights.

Dedicated to the Sun God

Chhath is mainly characterized by riverside rituals in which the Sun God, or Surya, is worshipped. It underpins the belief that the Sun God fulfills every wish of earthlings and so it's our duty to thank the sun with a special prayer for bestowing living beings with the gift of life. The ghats or riverbanks are filled with devotees as they come to complete their ritual worship or *arghya* of the sun – both at dawn and dusk. The morning 'arghya' is a prayer for a good harvest, peace and prosperity in the new year and the evening 'arghya' is an expression of thanks to the benevolence of the Sun God for all that he has bestowed during the year gone by.

How Chhath is Celebrated

Chhath can well be regarded as the state festival of Bihar, where it goes on for four days. Outside of India, Chhath is mainly celebrated by the Bhojpuri- and Maithili-speaking community apart from the Nepalese Hindus. People dress up in their best clothes and gather by rivers and other water bodies. Many devotees take a holy dip at dawn before preparing the ritual offerings or *prasad*, which mainly comprise '*thekua*,' a hard and crude but tasty wheat-based cake usually cooked on traditional earthen ovens called 'chulhas'. Women adorn new clothes, light lamps and sing devotional folk songs in honor of Chhat Maiya or the holy river Ganga. After sunset, devotees return home to celebrate Kosi when diyas are lit in the courtyard of the house and kept beneath a bower of sugarcane sticks. Serious devotees maintain a strict fast for three days with no food or even water.

The Four Days of Chhath

The first day of Chhath is called Nahai Khai, which literally means 'bath and eat'. Devotees bathe in the river and bring home the water to cook food offerings for the Sun God.

On the second day called Kharna, the devotees observe eight to twelve hours of fast without water and end it in the evening after performing puja.

The third day is also spent in worship while fasting without water. This day is marked by the elaborate evening ritual called the Sandhya Arghya or 'evening offering'. The offerings are served to the setting sun on bamboo trays that has *thekua*, coconut, and banana among other fruits. They chant the Beej Mantra prayer while doing so:

Om Hraam, Hreem, Hroum, Swaha, Suryaya Namah.

The fourth day of Chhath is considered the most auspicious when the final morning ritual or Bihaniya Arghya is performed. Devotees congregate on the bank of the river to offer *arghya*s to the rising sun. Once the morning ritual is over, devotees break their fast by taking a bite of ginger with sugar. This marks the end of the rituals as celebrations begin.

ACTIVITIES

1 TORAN FOR GOOD LUCK

Make a beautiful toran to hang on your doorway.

You Need:

- Sewing thread or *kalava* • 15–20 mango leaves
- Marigold flowers • Needle • A pair of scissors

Make It!

1) Take a thread or kalava long enough to cover the horizontal length of your doorway.
2) Attach the mango leaves to the thread using the petiole (the thin stem at the tip of the leaves). You can tie the thread around the petioles.

3) Leave a few centimetres of space between each leaf.
4) Your mango leaf toran is ready. However, if an adult agrees to help you with it, you can make one with marigold flowers to add a dash of colour.
5) Take another thread of the same length.
6) Tie a thick knot at one end of the thread so the flowers don't slip away.
7) Use a needle to pierce the free end of the thread through the flowers.
8) You can add as many flowers as you want as long as the thread can support them.
9) After that, tie up the free end of the thread.
10) You may wrap your marigold toran around your mango leaf toran or you may hang them separately.

2 AN OFFERING OF LIGHT

Decorate a tray of diyas that can be used in your Chhath Puja ceremonies.

You Need:

• Round leaf or foil bowls • 5-6 small mud diyas • Marigold flower petals • Round cotton wicks • A big plate or tray

Make It!

1) Keep one bowl in the centre of the plate/tray and keep the other bowls around it.
2) Sprinkle all the bowls with flower petals. Fill the one in the centre generously.

3) Keep mud diyas in all the bowls except the one in the centre.
4) Add one or two cotton wicks to each diya.
5) Ask an adult to add oil to the diyas and light them.

3 SHAPE-SHIFTING SUN

Let us celebrate the Sun God.

You Need:

• A drawing notebook • Sketch pens or markers

Make It!

The idea is to make different suns out of different shapes.

1) Draw a square and fill it up with colour.
2) Draw little rectangular rays emerging from its four edges.
3) Make more rectangle rays around the rest of the 'sun' but don't let these rays touch the main square.
4) Repeat the steps with a triangle and triangular rays.
5) Then, make a circular spiral for the sun's body and play with the shape of the rays.
6) You can also make the spiral angled so it's not completely circular.

4 CHHATH DESSERTS

Suggest these sweet recipes to your family. Adjust the ingredients according to the number of people.

Rice Kheer

You Need:

• ¼ cup basmati rice • Full-fat milk • Saffron
• Sliced almonds, cashews and other nuts • Sugar

Make It!

1) Rinse and soak the rice in water for a few minutes.
2) Cook one litre of full-fat milk on low heat. Let an adult oversee this stage as the milk boils.
3) Separate one tablespoon of this milk into a bowl and add a few strands of saffron to it.
4) Drain the rice and add it to the boiled milk. Mix it.
5) Cook it on low heat.
6) When the rice is halfway done, add sugar as per your taste. Mix and cook.
7) Add almonds, cashews and any other nuts that you like.
8) Add the saffron milk.
9) Mix and cook till the kheer thickens.
10) Serve it hot.

Thekua

You Need:

• 3 tbsp melted ghee • ½ cup chopped jaggery
• Salt • Wheat flour • *Saunf* (fennel)
• Grated coconut • Cardamom powder

Make It!

1) Whisk together about 150 gms of wheat flour with salt, *saunf*, grated coconut and cardamom powder.
2) Add hot ghee and mix.
3) Mix jaggery with a little bit of water and heat it until the jaggery melts.
4) Gradually add the jaggery solution to the flour mixture to create a dough. Let an adult supervise this process.
5) Knead the dough lightly to make it semi-soft.
6) Make flat biscuits from the dough.
7) You can use a small stick or toothpick to make patterns on the biscuits.
8) Ask an adult to fry the *thekua* until they are crisp.
9) Share them with your loved ones.

GURU NANAK JAYANTI

Gurparav or Guru Nanak Jayanti is the celebration of the birth of the founder of Sikhism.

Born in 1469, Guru Nanak Dev's life wasn't an extraordinary one. At a young age, he embarked on a spiritual odyssey, exploring diverse faiths and philosophies. Then, at the age of thirty, standing in the waters of the Kali Bein river, Nanak experienced the celestial sound of 'Ek Onkar', the primal mantra of oneness. This started him on his journey towards the luminous path of truth.

The Five Pillars of Sikhism

The five pillars of Sikhism provide a roadmap to spiritual liberation. Naam Japa is chanting the lord's name. Kirat Karni is the honest work that enriches everyone. Vand Chakna is about sharing meals in open kitchens. It dissolves social hierarchies and brings about a sense of belonging. Sattvic Jeevan means always remaining truthful and pure. And Simran is the meditation one does to connect with God.

How Sikhs Celebrate Gurparav

Gurdwaras or Sikh temples across the globe awaken to the melodious echoes of hymns and prayers on Gurparav. The Akhand Path, the continuous recitation of the holy book Guru Granth Sahib, fills the air.

Nagar Kirtan processions take place on streets, where devotees spread the Guru Nanak's message of unity.

But the essence of Gurparav is more than rituals and celebrations. It's embodied in the iconic 'Guru Ka Langar', a communal kitchen where free meals are served to all, irrespective of caste, creed or social status. This is the heart of Sikhism – a manifestation of selfless service, a testament to the oneness of humanity, a beacon of compassion in a world often shrouded in darkness.

The Golden Temple: Where Devotion Bathes in Light

No mention of Sikh celebrations can be complete without the Golden Temple in Amritsar. On Gurparav, the holy city is decorated to welcome all pilgrims. The glistening gold Darbar Sahib is bathed in the soft glow of lamps. It's like a special and peaceful place that makes people feel close to a divine connection. Devotees in vibrant attire dip their heads in the sacred waters of the temple's holy Sarovar, or pool. They seek the lord's blessings. The Langar Hall offers a feast for everyone, irrespective of faith or background, further adding to the festive spirit.

Across India, iconic gurdwaras like Gurdwara Sis Ganj Sahib in Delhi, Takht Damdama Sahib in Punjab, and Hazur Sahib in Maharashtra witness vibrant celebrations.

In Punjab, the land of Guru Nanak's birth, processions carry decorated palanquins bearing the Guru Granth Sahib. Traditional dancers and martial artistes join the procession and show their respect and devotion. Many devotees visit Gurdwara Kartarpur Sahib, the historic site across the border in Pakistan, where Guru Nanak spent his final years.

Beyond Borders: Gurparav Resonates Globally

Gurdwaras around the world, from England to Canada to Australia, echo with the echoes of hymns and prayers on Guru Nanak Jayanti. Gurparav becomes a platform not just for celebration but for connecting with the Sikh diaspora. Sikhs share the Guru's timeless message of universal love, selfless service and honest living.

ACTIVITIES

1 KADA PRASAD

Help prepare an important prasad served in gurudwaras all over the country.

You Need:

- 1 cup sugar • 1 cup wheat flour
- Ghee

Make It!

1) Add sugar to a saucepan along with three cups of water.
2) Under an adult's charge, heat it for a few minutes until the sugar dissolves. Let it come to a boil.
3) Melt one cup of ghee in a *kadai* and then add whole wheat flour.
4) Ask an adult to fry the flour till it turns golden brown.

5) Once that is done, start adding the sugar syrup slowly.
6) Keep stirring it while you cook it.
7) Cook till the prasad becomes semi-thick.
8) Serve it hot!

2 DECIPHER A MANTRA

A well-known mantra given by Guru Nanak Deva is given below, along with the translations of a few words. Try to figure out the meaning behind the whole mantra. 'Ik oa(n)kaar sath naam kartha purakh nirbhau nirvair akaal moorath ajuni saibha(n) gur prasaadh II'

Ik = one
Sath = truth
Naam = name
Kartha = creator
Nirbhau = fearless
Vair = hate
Kaal = time
Ajuni = unborn
Saibha(n) = self-existent
Prasaadh = grace

3 COLOUR THE TEMPLE GOLDEN

Try a new way of adding colour and gold to the Golden Temple.

You Need:

• A printed outline of the temple • Golden paper • Blue paper • Glue

Make It!

1) Get the printout beforehand.
2) Tear out small bits of the golden and blue sheets of paper.
3) Paste the golden bits on the image of the temple and the blue bits below it to denote water.
4) Attach the final picture with this activity as a token of your art.

4 FIVE KS

The five Ks are five items Guru Gobind Singh commanded the Khalsa Sikhs to wear at all times. See if you can unscramble the words and find them.

1) sehk ____________________

2) ghanka ____________________

3) akar ____________________

4) kaercha ____________________

5) riknap ____________________

5 TEST YOUR KNOWLEDGE

Rearrange Column B to correctly match with the expressions in Column A.

Column A	Column B
1. Another name of Guru Nanak	a. Guru Granth Sahib
2. Holy Scripture	b. Kali Bein
3. Nanak is said to have died in	c. Baba Nanak
4. The river Nanak bathed in before enlightenment	d. Narowal, Pakistan

Answers:

1) kesh, 2) kangha, 3) kara, 4) kachera, 5) kirpan

Answers:

1) c, 2) a, 3) b, 4) d

CHRISTMAS

The Word

Christmas, which comes from the Old English phrase 'Cristes mæsse', or festival of Christ, is celebrated as the birth of Jesus Christ.

The Date

The Bible doesn't tell us anything about the day or year of Christ's birth. However, it is generally believed that Jesus was born sometime between 7 BCE and 4 BCE.

About 350 CE, 25 December was chosen by Pope Julius I as the date of 'Nativity' or Christ's birthday.

The Nativity Story

The story of Jesus' birth dates back more than 2,000 years in the town of Nazareth in Israel. A young woman called Mary was engaged to a carpenter called Joseph. One day, the angel Gabriel appeared before Mary and said that she would soon become the mother of a very special baby and that she should name him Jesus.

Soon after the couple was married, the Roman Emperor Augustus passed a law whereby all Jews had to register themselves in their place of birth. Thus, Mary and Joseph had to go on a long journey to Joseph's hometown, Bethlehem. When they arrived, the city was so crowded that Mary and Joseph could not find any place to spend the night. Finally, an innkeeper allowed them to stay in his stable for the night. This is where Mary gave birth to her son a few hours later. As there was no bed for the baby, she wrapped him in cloth and laid him in a manger filled with hay to keep him warm.

At the time of Jesus' birth, some shepherds near a hillside in Bethlehem saw a bright light appear in the sky. It was an angel sent by God to share the good news about the birth of Jesus. Hearing this auspicious news, the shepherds went to see the baby. When they arrived at the stable, they knelt down to pray to baby Jesus. They told Mary and Joseph the story of the angel and revealed that Jesus was no ordinary boy but the son of God.

ALL ABOUT SANTA CLAUS

Christmas reminds us of that jolly old man with a white beard, a flowing red suit and a big sack of goodies – Santa Claus. The name 'Santa Claus' comes from the fourth century Greek gift-giver and miracle-maker, St. Nicholas. In 1823, Clement Clarke Moore wrote a Christmas poem called 'A Visit from St. Nicholas'.

Inspired by Moore's poem, Thomas Nast, an American cartoonist, came up with a caricature of Santa Claus, which gave the merry old man his physical attributes. And so was born the burly grandfather-like character with red and white fur-lined clothes and hat. Nast's version of Santa gave Santa a home near the North Pole and a mode of transport – a sleigh pulled by eight flying reindeer, including Rudolph, who had a red nose. The sleigh is sometimes followed by many magical elves. Along with Santa and his reindeer came the custom of filling up stockings with presents on the night of Christmas Eve and the idea of Santa secretly entering homes through chimneys at night.

Today, Santa Claus is a much-loved character and is well known around the world. In England, Santa's name is Father Christmas. In France, he is known as Pere Noel. In Germany, he is called Christkindl or Christ Child. And in China, Santa Claus is called Shengdan Laoren.

The Real Santa Claus Village

Santa's home is said to be in Finland's Lapland region. The Santa Claus village near Rovaniemi in southern Lapland has become the top tourist destination in Finland.

Visitors can see Santa's office and his magical cave where cute little elves will invite you in for a chat with Santa Claus and take a photograph with him.

You can also cross the Arctic Circle here, and even send a letter home from Santa's Post Office. You can choose your Santa Claus postcard and send home Christmas greetings with a unique Santa Claus postmark.

Write a Letter to Santa

When kids come to know that Santa would be visiting their home with gifts on Christmas Eve, they write letters to him with their choice of Christmas presents. It is a custom to place letters near the fireplace or on the mantle for Santa to come and read them.

You too can write to Santa by sending an email at CanadaPost.ca. And yes, you will get a reply from Santa Claus.

THE CHRISTMAS TREE

The tradition of setting up a Christmas tree has its roots in sixteenth century Germany. There people decorated a fir tree on Christmas Eve with apples to remember Adam and Eve in the Garden of Eden. Over time, other decorative items such as stars, candles and ornaments were added to it, and the Christmas tree, as we know it, was born. Legend goes that it was a German called Martin Luther who brought the tree indoors. As he was returning home one wintry night, he saw the stars twinkling in the sky through branches of a fir tree. Charmed by the sight, Martin Luther went into the woods and got himself a small fir tree. He then took it indoors and decorated it with candles, which represented the stars he had seen. This custom spread in Germany and then all over the world.

Christmas Decorations

All kinds of decorations are used to brighten up the Christmas tree and the home during this time. The main colours of this festival are red, green and white as well as gold and silver.

The Star

Traditionally, either a star or an angel is placed at the top of the tree. The star represents the Star of Bethlehem which first revealed the news of Christ's birth to three astrologers called the Three Wise Men and then led them to baby Jesus in Bethlehem.

Tinsel

The Christmas tree is often decorated with silvery strips called 'tinsel'. Long ago, there was a woman who was so poor that she had no money to decorate the Christmas tree for her children. She prayed that her children would not feel too unhappy about their tree. And someone actually heard her prayers.

That night when they went to sleep, spiders landed on the bare tree and wove cobwebs all over it. When the children woke in the morning, they saw their tree covered in fine cobwebs that shone like silver in the moonlight. And so tinsel started being used to decorate all Christmas trees.

Holly Leaves

The evergreen holly tree with pretty pointed leaves and clusters of bright red berries is said to represent the life and death of Jesus Christ. The holly is connected to the Crucifixion of Christ and his death, after being tried and sentenced by the Roman prefect, Pontius Pilate. The thorny leaves symbolize the crown of thorns that was placed on his head before the Crucifixion. The red berries represent drops of blood that spilled from his wounds when he was nailed to the cross. The evergreen leaves are said to symbolize eternal life and Christ's resurrection or rebirth from the grave.

Mistletoe

Mistletoe was used by Druids (Celtic priests of the pre-Christian era) 200 years before the birth of Christ in their winter celebrations. This plant was worshipped because of its remarkable properties: it had no roots, yet it remained green during the winter months. The ancient Celts also believed mistletoe was an antidote for poison and kept evil spirits away.

Scandinavians associated the plant with Frigga, their Goddess of Love. It may be from this that the custom of kissing under the mistletoe is derived. It is believed that those who kissed under the mistletoe were blessed with happiness and good luck and possibly a wedding in the following year.

ACTIVITIES

1 STANDALONE CHRISTMAS STAR

You Need:

• Printer (optional) • Stiff paper (like card stock, thick chart paper or thin cardboard) or Styrofoam trays • A pair of scissors • Crayons or markers

Make It!

1) Two paper stars are needed to make one three-dimensional star. Draw two identical 5-pointed stars of the exact same size on a piece of stiff paper.
2) Cut out the stars and then decorate them on both sides. If you don't want to decorate them, you can just use coloured paper. The traditional Christmas colours are red and green; you could use one of each.
3) Make one slit in each star. In one star, the slit is through an inner corner between two points till the centre of the star. In the other, the slit through an outer corner till the centre.

4) Slip the two stars together through the slits. For stability, you may have to tape the stars a bit where they meet at the slits.
5) You now have a three-dimensional star decoration that stands by itself on a table.

2 PAPER CHRISTMAS TREE

Make a simple three-dimensional Christmas tree from construction paper. These trees look great sitting on the mantle or on a windowsill.

You Need:

• Green construction paper or chart paper • Crayons, markers, glitter glue • A pair of scissors • Clear tape • Optional: Other colours of construction paper, glue, hole punch, stickers

Make It!

1) Fold a piece of green construction paper in half and then cut it in half.
2) Place the two pieces one on top of another and fold them in half again.
3) Draw half a Christmas tree on either side along the fold.
4) Unfold the papers and cut out the outline of a tree.
5) Fold the papers in half again, this time horizontally in order to mark the centre of the tree with a pencil.

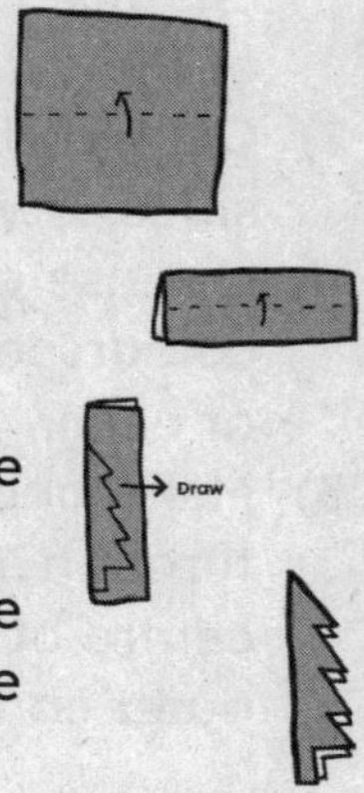

6) On one tree, make a slit from the top of the tree running through the middle till the centre. On the other, make the slit from the bottom, running through the middle to the centre.

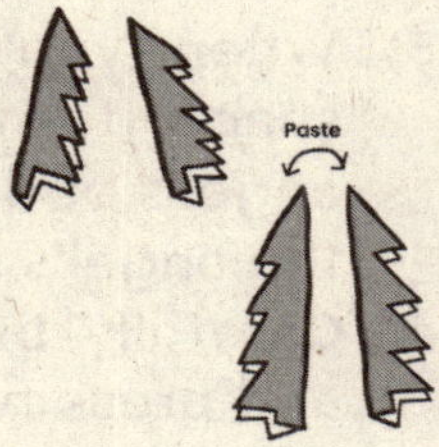

7) Slip the two trees together along the slits. Using clear tape, tape the bottoms and tops together.

8) Decorate your tree with crayons, markers or glitter glue. Or you can glue on tiny construction paper decorations or use star stickers. You can cut out tiny paper balls using a hole punch. Now you have a really nice three-dimensional Christmas decoration.

3 EDIBLE ANGELS

You Need:

• 1 cup peanut butter • 1 cup honey • 2½ cups powdered milk • Waffle cones • Thin liquorice string • Raisins • Coloured gems

Make It!

1) To make the clay, put peanut butter, honey and powdered milk in a big bowl.
2) Squeeze and knead the ingredients together. If the clay is too sticky, add a little more powdered milk. If it is too dry, add a little more honey or peanut butter.

3) When you have nice, smooth-feeling clay, shape it into a three-inch cone to make the angel's body. Add a little ball of clay on top for the angel's head.
4) Carefully break off parts of the waffle cone and press two pieces into the angel's back for wings.
5) Wind some liquorice string around the head for a halo.
6) Stick raisins on the head for eyes and gems on the body for some colour. Your yummy angel is ready to fly into your tummy!

4 BROWN PAPER STOCKING

Make a great Christmas stocking from a brown paper grocery bag. You can hang it from your mantle and stuff it with Christmas goodies.

You Need:

• Thick brown paper (like carry bag paper)
• Pencil • A pair of scissor • Glue • A hole puncher
• Yarn • Markers or crayons

Make It!

1) Draw a large stocking on thick brown paper.
2) Cut out two copies of this stocking.
3) Punch holes around the edges of the stocking.
4) Weave yarn in and out of the holes. Leave a loop of yarn at one end and tie it in a knot.

5) Decorate your stocking with crayons, markers, stickers, construction paper cut-outs or glitter.

5 CHRISTMAS CHARADES

You Need:

• Chits of paper • A pen • A bowl

Play It!

1) Make a list of Christmas-related themes, such as names of carols, holiday traditions and popular Christmas movies.
2) Write them down on chits of paper. Place them in a bowl.
3) Take turns picking out a chit and acting out the words with gestures while remaining completely silent.

6 PAPER PLATE SNOWMAN

You Need:

• Two white paper plates • Construction paper (black, red) or wrapping paper • An orange tube or carrot end (for the nose) • A short length of ribbon • Hole punch • Marker or crayons • A pair of scissors • Glue • Optional: Googly eyes, button

Make It!

1) On one of the paper plates, cut off the outer rim, making a smaller plate.

2) Punch a hole near the rim on both plates.
3) Tie the two plates together using the ribbon.
4) On black construction paper, draw and then cut out a top hat and two boots. On coloured construction paper, draw and then cut out two gloves.
5) Glue the hat, boots and gloves on the snowman. Either glue on googly eyes or draw eyes. Draw a mouth. For the nose, cut a short length from an orange tube. Stick the tube through the plate to secure it.
6) For the buttons, you can cut out shapes from construction paper, use round stickers, glue on real buttons, or simply draw them.

You now have a cute snowman decoration!

7 CHRISTMAS TONGUE TWISTERS

You Need:

Silly Christmas tongue twisters

Play It!

Say each phrase three times as fast as you can. A candy prize for anyone who tries. There are some examples below but you can let your imagination run wild and come up with phrases that your own.

- Santa sings super songs on starry stairs
- Santa skis over snowy slopes to save some time
- Big bright bells bring bubbling bags of smiles
- Grumpy Grinch gets grizzled and grouchy
- Pretty packed presents and poodles in pink

- Sally's striped stocking swinging from the sleigh
- Santa's super sleigh swiftly slides sideways
- Cheery carols with Christmas cookies and candy cane caps

Colour me!

NEW YEAR CELEBRATIONS

Celebrating the New Year in India can vary depending on where you are. The festivities may have different names. The activities may change. And they may even be celebrated on different days. Although the Indian national calendar is the official calendar for country, regional variants strongly prevail. As a result, there are a host of new year celebrations that are unique to various regions. Most of these major springtime festivities are held in March or April.

Ugadi in Andhra Pradesh and Karnataka

If you are in the southern Indian states of Andhra Pradesh and Karnataka, then you will hear the story about Lord Brahma, who began the creation of the universe on Ugadi. People prepare for the New Year by cleaning their home and buying new clothes. On Ugadi Day, they decorate their home with mango leaves and rangoli designs. They pray for a prosperous New Year, and visit temples to listen to the yearly calendar, the *Panchangasravanam*, as priests make predictions for the coming year. Ugadi is an auspicious day to embark on a new journey.

Gudi Padwa in Maharashtra and Goa

In Maharashtra and Goa, the New Year is celebrated as Gudi Padwa. The festival heralds the advent of spring. Early on the morning of the first day of the Chaitra month, people wear new clothes and decorate their homes with colourful rangoli patterns. A silk banner is raised and worshipped, while greetings and sweets are exchanged. People hang a gudi on their windows, a decorated pole with a brass or a silver vessel placed on it, to celebrate Mother Nature's bounty.

Cheti Chand for the Sindhis

For New Year's Day, Sindhis celebrate Cheti Chand, which is similar to Thanksgiving Day. Cheti Chand falls on the first day of the month of Chaitra, which is called Cheti in Sindhi. This day is observed as the birthday of Jhulelal, the patron saint of the Sindhis. On this day, Sindhis worship Varuna, the water god, and observe a number of rituals followed by feasts and devotional music such as *bhajans* and aartis.

Baisakhi, the Punjabi New Year

Baisakhi, traditionally a harvest festival, is celebrated on April 13 or 14 every year, marking the Punjabi New Year.

To ring in the New Year, people celebrate by performing the bhangra and *giddha* dances to the pounding rhythm of the *dhol* drum. Historically, Baisakhi also marks the founding of the Sikh Khalsa warriors by Guru Gobind Singh in the late seventeenth century.

Poila Baishakh in Bengal

The first day of the Bengali New Year falls between April 13 and 15 every year. This special day is called Poila Baishakh. It is a state holiday in the eastern state of West Bengal and a national holiday in Bangladesh. The New Year, called Naba Barsha, is a time for people to clean and decorate their houses and invoke Lakshmi, the goddess of wealth and prosperity. All new enterprises start on this auspicious day. Businessmen open their fresh ledgers with Haal Khata, a ceremony in which Lord Ganesha is summoned and customers are invited to settle all their old dues. The people of Bengal spend the day feasting and participating in cultural activities.

Bohag Bihu or Rongali Buhu in Assam

Assam ushers in the New Year with the spring festival of Bohag Bihu or Rongali Bihu. It marks the onset of a new agricultural cycle. While Bohag denotes the Assamese calendar, Rongali is the name of the annual festival showcasing the tribal culture of the state. Fairs are organized in which people revel in fun and games. Young women in traditional attire sing Bihu *geet* and dance the traditional *mukoli* Bihu. People visit each other's homes, wish them well in the New Year and exchange gifts and sweets. The festive food of the occasion is *pitha* or rice cakes.

Vishu in Kerala

Vishu is the first day in the first month of Medam in Kerala. The people of this state begin the day early by visiting the temple and looking for an auspicious sight called Vishukani. It includes golden flowers, fruits and vegetables, mirror, clothes, gold coins and an image of Lord Krishna. It is believed that the new year will be better if one views auspicious joyful items such as Vishukani as the first thing on Vishu. The day is full of elaborate traditional rituals with token coins called *vishukaineetam* distributed among the needy. People wear new clothes, *kodi vastram*, and celebrate the day by bursting firecrackers and enjoying an elaborate lunch called *sadya* with family and friends. The afternoon and evening are spent at a Vishuvela or festival.

Varsha Pirappu or Puthandu Vazthukal, the Tamil New Year

Tamil-speaking people across the globe celebrate Varsha Pirappu or Puthandu Vazthukal, the Tamil New Year, in mid-April. It is the first day of Chithirai, which is the first month in the traditional Tamil calendar. The day dawns by observing *kanni* or viewing propitious things, such as gold, silver, jewellery, new clothes, new calendar, rice, coconuts, fruits, vegetables, and other fresh products. This ritual is believed to usher in good fortune. The morning includes a ritualistic bath and almanac worship called *panchanga* puja. The Tamil Panchangam, a book on New Year predictions, is decorated with sandalwood and turmeric paste, flowers and vermilion powder, and is placed before the deity. Later, it is read or listened to either at home or at the temple.

On the eve of Puthandu, doorways are garlanded with mango leaves strung together and *vilakku kolam* decorative patterns adorn the floors. Donning new clothes, the family members gather and light a traditional lamp, the *kuthu vilakku*, and fill *niraikudum*, a short-necked brass bowl with water, and embellish it with mango leaves while chanting prayers. The traditional Puthandu meal consists of *pachadi*, a mixture of jaggery, chilies, salt, neem leaf or flowers and tamarind, plus a green banana and jackfruit concoction as well as a variety of sweet *payasam* desserts.

Navroz, the Parsi New Year

Navroz, the Parsi New Year, is marked by joyous activities that brings the Parsi community together. 'Nav-roz' literally means 'new day'. As per the Shahenshahi calendar followed by the Parsi community in India, Navroz is usually celebrated around mid-August. It marks the victory of light over darkness, as the legend tells of the prophet Zoroaster receiving divine revelation on this day.

In Parsi places of worship, called Fire Temples, sacred fires flicker at altars. A few special items are offered to the prophet: pomegranates symbolizing life, coins symbolizing prosperity, and bowls filled with rosewater, a reminder of purity. The beats of drums and the melodies of *kusti* prayers fill the air as families gather for blessings. Elders bless the young and share stories of their ancestors and rich heritage. Parsis enjoy Navroz specialties like *dhansak*, a meat stew fragrant with spices, and *falooda*, a sweet vermicelli pudding.

ACTIVITIES

1 ADORN YOUR VISHU KANI

Practise the customs of Vishu with some art and craft.

You Need:

- A plain hand mirror
- Newspapers and magazines
- Glue

Make It!

1) With just your hands, tear out small bits of coloured paper from old newspapers and magazines. A variety of colours and textures would be even better.
2) Once you have enough bits of paper, start glueing them to the outer rim of your hand mirror.
3) Use very little glue to avoid making a mess.
4) If the mirror doesn't have a rim thick enough for you to decorate, you can paste the bits on the outer boundary of the glass.
5) Let it dry for some time, then add your decorated mirror to the Vishukani.

2 MINI GUDI

Make a mini version of a special Gudi Padwa symbol.

You Need:

• An unsharpened pencil • Yarn • Colourful beads • Cotton • Neem or small mango leaves • Mini pot or a ceramic mug • A small piece of fabric or a small handkerchief • Playdough • A small copper/brass pot or kalasha

Make It!

1) Take a piece of yarn big enough to make a small garland.
2) Knot one end of it and start adding beads to it. Try to use red, yellow or orange beads to signify flowers.
3) After that, take the free end of the yarn and tie both ends together.
4) Take another piece of yarn of the same length.
5) Tear out tiny balls of cotton and stick them to this yarn.
6) Tie the two ends together to make another garland.
7) Put one end of the pencil inside your mini pot and seal it in there using playdough. Let the pencil tilt a little to one side.

8) Put your chosen fabric on top of the pencil. Place the garlands and leaves here and tie everything up with yarn so it doesn't fall off.
9) Place the *kalasha* upside down on top of this arrangement and your mini Gudi is ready.

3 DELIGHT YOUR BIHU TASTEBUDS

Prepare an Assamese breakfast for your loved ones! Keep in mind that the ingredients given below are enough for one person.

You Need:

- 2 mashed potatoes
- Half of a sliced onion
- 1 green chilli
- Minced coriander leaves
- Mustard Oil
- Salt

Make It!

1) Ask an adult to boil the potatoes and slice the chilli beforehand.
2) Peel the boiled potatoes and mash them well. Don't leave any lumps of potato.
3) Mix the mashed potatoes with mustard oil, chillis and about half a teaspoon of salt.
4) Garnish your breakfast with coriander leaves.

4 BATHE YOUR HOME IN BAISAKHI HUES

There are multiple ways to decorate your doorways and windows with the bright colours of Baisakhi.

You Need:

• Red, yellow and orange dupattas • Safety pins

Decorate It!

1) You can use red or orange dupattas to curtain your windows. Secure one end of the dupatta around your curtain rod using safety pins. Tie a yellow dupatta around the middle of this curtain.
2) You may also intertwine or twist together dupattas of three colours and then use the piece as a garland or *bandhanwar*.
3) If your home has a designated place of worship, you can add colour to it by decorating its entrance or frame by wrapping dupattas around it.

5 UGADI CENTREPIECE

Add a festive tinge to your living room table with a simple DIY centrepiece.

You Need:

• Mango leaves • Marigold flowers
• A ceramic or glass plate

Make It!

1) Lay out the mango leaves on a plate in a floral pattern. The leaves here become the petals.
2) Keep four to five marigold flowers in the centre where all the leaves meet.

3) You may tear out the petals of a few remaining flowers and fill up the empty spaces between the leaves.
4) Place the plate carefully on the table where everyone can see it.

6 CHETI CHAND PRASAD

Prepare a delicious mint chutney to pair with a traditional flatbread called Dhodho.

You Need:

• 2 cups mint leaves • Green chilli
• Chopped ginger
• Salt • Dry mango powder • Cumin powder
• Black salt • ½ tsp lemon juice

Make It!

1) Add all the ingredients to a blender, one by one.
2) Let an adult help you with the measurements of salt and other spices.
3) Add the lemon juice last of all.
4) Add a few drops of water and blend.
5) Scoop the chutney out into a bowl or jar, and serve to your family.

7 POILA BAISAKH MASQUERADE

Take part in new year festivities with a hand-made Poila Baisakh mask that can later be used as simple decor.

You Need:

• Balloons • Newspaper • Glue • Water
• Bowl • Paintbrushes • Paints
• A pair of scissors • Markers

Make It!

1) Make a papier-mâché paste with one part glue and two parts water. Mix it with a paintbrush.
2) Inflame a balloon or ask someone to do it for you. Tie it up so the air doesn't escape.
3) Using your papier-mâché paste, stick small bits of newspaper on the balloon's surface all around.
4) Add two or three layers of newspaper bits to make the final product sturdy.
5) Let it dry for at least half an hour.
6) With a scissor, carefully puncture the balloon and remove it from the papier-mâché structure.
7) Only cut out the part of the structure that you would need for your mask.
8) Draw a face on your mask. Many people carry owl masks during Poila Baisakh processions but you can also draw a human face.
9) Paint it with different colours, but try to use red and white as much as possible.
10) Let it dry and then show it to your friends.

8 PROMISES OF VARUSHA PIRAPPU

Gather your friends and distribute blank pages and pens amongst yourselves. Write down any five New Year

Resolutions, that is, goals you wish to achieve in the coming year, on your respective sheets. Discuss your resolutions and plan out ways to make them come true.

Record your resolutions down below so you do not forget them.

____

____

____

____

____

9 PAINT A BONFIRE

Commemorate the fire temples of Zoroastrianism with a fun, creative way to paint fire.

You Need:

• White sheet of paper • Yellow, red and orange paints • Tissues

Make It!

1) Let out a little yellow paint in the bottom-centre of your white sheet.
2) Scrunch up a clean tissue and use it to spread the paint out to look like flames.

3) Repeat the steps with orange and red paints. Remember to use less red to avoid a final colour becoming too dark.
4) Let the colours mix and surprise yourself with a beautiful final painting.
5) You may cut it out and paste it below as a token of your artistic skills.